# HOME IS WHERE THE HEART IS

*Book 2 of the Harbor Cove Series*

## LAUREL WENSON

*I dedicate this book with love & gratitude to*

*Melissa Koberlein*
*Author, mentor, and friend*

*Thank you for pushing me*
*to bring my dreams to life,*
*and for sharing the journey.*

Welcome to Gloucester, MA! While this is a work of fiction, the story takes place in a real setting.

Gloucester has been special to me all my life. As a child, our extended family would picnic at Stage Fort Park, and my cousins and I would climb the rocks on Half Moon Beach and Tablet Rock. I toured Hammond Castle, fascinated by the Great Room, the courtyard, and the gorgeous gothic arches overlooking the harbor. My dad's love of boats prompted many visits to the harbor along Stacy Boulevard and Rodgers Street, and I have vivid memories of walking along Pavilion Beach and wondering what the Greasy Pole platform out in the harbor was all about. We walked along the State Pier and around Harbor Cove to admire countless fishing boats, and enjoyed fresh seafood at Woodman's in nearby Essex.

As a young adult, I'd join friends for beach trips to Good Harbor or Wingersheek, and on my own, I spent countless hours perched out on the breakwater at Eastern Point, or staying overnight at the Cape Ann Motor Inn on Long Beach. Although I haven't been back in many years, I will always love this small fishing community, and it was an easy choice as my series location.

You will find real places and events mentioned in the series. There is an actual neighborhood known as the "Fort" between Pavilion Beach and Harbor Cove, and documentaries exist to give the history of how it came to be one big "family". Every June, there's a wonderful fiesta in honor of St. Peter, and the Greasy Pole contest is a highlight of the weekend. Across the harbor, Hammond Castle is still open to the public for tours of magnificent medieval architecture. Along the way, the Fishermen's Monument stands proudly facing the harbor in memory of those who have been lost at sea.

While several locations in the story are real, this is a work of fiction. Please know that some places may not be described exactly as they are in real life. None of the characters are real people, and the story ideas all come from my imagination. I hope you enjoy the melding of "real" places with "make believe" characters -- Viva!

To learn more about Gloucester, visit: discovergloucester.com

# CHAPTER ONE

Half of Elena's BLT sandwich remained on the plate, and Carla blamed a dead man. Once Jeopardy started, her grandmother left the dinner table and headed for the living room to watch her favorite show, no matter what.

*She doesn't even realize it's not Alex Trebek anymore. At least she finished her soup – and I can make her a snack before bed.* She debated wrapping up the sandwich for later, but instead took a bite as she cleared her nonna's dishes. The saltiness of the bacon mingled with the juices of the tomato, and she ate more. *No sense in letting it go to waste – she won't remember leaving it anyway.*

She wiped down the table and washed the dishes, with the theme song in the next room signaling a commercial break. No matter how bad the dementia got, Nonna still recognized the Jeopardy theme song after years of watching every evening. *Thank God for Jeopardy; I get my guaranteed half hour of peace every night after working all day.* With the last utensil in the drying rack, Carla squeezed the remaining suds out of the sponge and dried her hands off. *Now I can enjoy the rest of my coffee.*

Before her first sip, her grandmother wandered back into the kitchen.

"Hey, Nonna, it's only a commercial. Jeopardy will be back—"

Something wasn't right. Her grandmother was leaning funny to one side, and holding her head with her hand. One side of her mouth drooped down, and guttural gibberish was all Nonna could manage.

"Nonna! What is it?" Carla dashed to her grandmother's side, lowering her onto one of the chairs while grabbing her phone from the middle of the table. Her grandmother continued leaning against her, and Carla suspected she'd fall to the floor if she didn't hold her up. *Oh, God, what do I do?* She dialed the only number she could think of – her neighbors across the street, who had been her chosen family for years.

Jean McBride picked up on the second ring. "Hey, neighbor; what's—"

"Something's wrong with Nonna!" Carla choked out. "Can you come over?"

"What's going on?"

"She's talkin' gibberish...and leaning funny...please come!"

Jean heard the panic in Carla's voice. "Look, I'm not home, but Hannah is. I want you to hang up and dial 911 right away, and I'll call Hannah to send her over."

"I don't know what's wrong with her!"

"Honey, it sounds like she might be having a stroke. Call the ambulance – Hannah will be over in a couple of minutes, so you won't be alone, I promise. I'll be there as soon as I can."

*A stroke? Oh, God...* She hung up the phone and dialed 911 with trembling fingers. "It's okay, Nonna, I'm gonna get you some help." She stroked her grandmother's hair, wondering how her frail body felt so heavy against her own.

"911. What is the nature of your emergency?"

Carla forced herself to keep her voice calm, even as the tears filled her eyes. She gave her name and address and shared the symptoms, finding some solace in the dispatcher's steady reply. "Help is on the way; do you need me to stay on the line with you until they arrive?"

Carla heard Hannah's approach outside the back door. "No, my best friend is here with me; I'm okay."

Hannah threw open the door as the tears finally spilled down Carla's cheeks. "Carla, I'm—"

Carla reached out her free arm for a needed hug. "She'll fall if I move...I'm so scared."

Hannah embraced her friend and the woman who had been an adopted grandmother. "The ambulance is almost here; I heard the siren as I rushed over." She reached down and squeezed Elena's hand. "You hang in there, Elena; help is on the way." She met her best friend's gaze, noting the fear in her eyes. "Just breathe, bestie. Is the front door unlocked?"

Carla shook her head. "I was lucky to get her into a chair."

"Are you okay for a minute if I open the door and get more lights on in the living room?"

Carla nodded, wiping her tears away with her free hand, never stopping the gentle strokes on her grandmother's hair. Elena continued odd guttural noises with an occasional word mixed in, but Carla noted only her right arm was moving at all at this point. "It's okay, Nonna. I won't leave you alone." *Please, dear God. Hurry. Don't let her die. I can't lose her yet.*

Hannah opened the door for the paramedics and police officer and led them to the kitchen. "Her name is Elena and she has dementia. This is her granddaughter Carla, who lives with her." As the paramedics took over, she circled around to Carla's side.

"She walked in, leaning to one side." Carla's speech was as fast as her heart pounding. "I sat her down....need to hold her up on this side."

A female paramedic with the name Haley on her badge stepped close to Carla as another named Andy knelt down on the other side of Elena's chair.

"I'm going to switch places with you." Haley's voice was calm and quiet. "You can stand right behind the chair if you want to keep talking to her, okay?"

Carla nodded as Andy greeted Elena and gently checked her vitals. "We're here to take care of you, Elena. Your granddaughter's right behind you, so you're in good hands."

"Is it a stroke?" Carla whispered.

"We can't say for sure," Haley replied, "But the signs suggest it.

We'll take her to the hospital right away. Can you tell the officer what happened while we get her ready, and then you can either ride in the ambulance or with your friend."

"I don't wanna leave her – she'll be confused."

"That's fine," said the police officer, who had been asking Hannah some questions. "I got all the information I need from your friend; I just need your phone number and then you can ride with your grandmother."

"I'll follow in my car," Hannah said. "And I'll call my mom to tell her to meet us there, okay?"

Carla nodded, knowing she had to step back to let the paramedics lift Nonna onto a gurney, but hating the distance between them. *Please, God...don't let her be afraid. I'm scared enough for both of us.*

———

Across the harbor, Jean ended her call to instant chaos.

Elena's daughter, Betty Sue Marino, had started right in when she heard the word "stroke."

"A stroke? An ambulance? Is it Mother?" She sat on the couch with Kelly Fitzgerald-Doyle sitting next to her.

Jean held up her hand as she dialed another number. As she instructed Hannah on what to do, Kelly squeezed Betty Sue's hand. "It'll be okay; we'll meet them at the hospital."

"Is it bad?"

Jean nodded as she stood up. "Betty Sue, we can all ride together, but we need to—"

"I'll drive her," Kelly said. "You take your car and head out now; we'll be right behind you. Carla needs you."

"What about me?" Betty Sue wailed. "I need you, too. Both of you!"

"Kelly will take good care of you," Jean said, grabbing her coat. "You'll only be a few minutes behind me."

# CHAPTER TWO

Jean arrived at the emergency room to find Carla and Hannah sitting by the window. She sat down on Carla's other side and wrapped her arm around her shoulder. "You okay?"

Carla's cheeks were still damp and puffy from crying, but she was calmer than she'd been on the phone. "They wouldn't let me go back with them; said they have to do tests."

"She's in good hands," Jean assured. "And they'll do everything they can." She looked over Carla's head to Hannah. "I'm so glad you were home."

"Me, too." Hannah glanced toward the door. "Where's Betty Sue? Didn't she come with you?"

Carla's head jerked up. "That's where you were? At my mom's?"

"I left right away. Kelly's driving her over – they should be here soon."

"Great...that's *all* I need," Carla groaned.

"She needs to be here – it's her mother."

"Why?" Carla asked. "It's not like she cares. She'll turn on her poor Southern Belle routine and make it all about her."

Jean kept her voice calm. "That might be true, but she still needs to be here."

"Besides," Hannah said, "The whole Southern Belle routine is part of who she is after all those years in Tennessee."

"I wish she had *stayed* there," Carla mumbled.

"We'll manage your mother," Jean said. "You concentrate on your nonna, okay?"

Carla nodded, her gaze darting to the automatic door leading to the back every time it opened. A nurse came out and called for someone else.

"It'll be a while," Hannah assured. "But brace yourself, because the Southern Belle has arrived."

True to form, Betty Sue entered through the sliding doors with tissue in hand and Kelly beside her to offer comfort. She rushed over to Jean. "Any word?"

She met Carla's gaze. "Why aren't you back there with her? Should she be alone?"

Before Carla could fly off the handle, Jean stood up and ushered Betty Sue and Kelly to the chairs just across from them. "She's having tests done; no one is allowed back yet. Can I get you some coffee?"

"Oh, I couldn't drink a thing," Betty Sue said, the southern drawl creeping back into her voice. "It's like sitting in the hospital all over again – back when my Kenneth died...only I was all alone down there." She patted Kelly's hand. "At least now I have my friends here to console me. Maybe you should call the others?"

Jean shook her head. "Let's wait until we have some news." She returned to her seat next to Carla, who had accurately predicted her mother's behavior.

Betty Sue met her gaze. "Everything'll be fine, Carla—don't worry 'bout Nonna."

Carla glared at her. "What does that even *mean*? Maybe *you're* not worried, with your buddies around you, but she's my *rock*, and we don't know how she is."

"Did it occur to you I might have been trying to be supportive?" Betty Sue's drawl had disappeared quickly.

Hannah rubbed Carla's back. "She's at least making an attempt," she whispered.

Carla leaned back, staring at her mother defiantly. "Only because your mom personally dragged her here. Otherwise, she'd still be home drinking with her friends."

"That's not fair!" Betty Sue retorted. "I can't believe—"

"Oh, come on, Mom! If your new boyfriend wasn't in jail, you wouldn't be here right now. Be honest for once."

"Will both of you *stop?*" Jean hissed. "I know you two have crap loads of issues to work through, but Elena needs *both* of you, so you're gonna have to figure out how to communicate with each other – and you both suck at it."

Carla watched as Betty Sue crumpled back in her chair, knowing her words had made an impact. *So now you know how it feels to be used by someone, don't you? That jerk would have cleaned your hefty bank account right out if it wasn't for your friends figuring out what a scumbag he was. You would've had to get a job and work your butt off – like I have all my life.*

They all sat in silence after Jean's scolding, with snippets of conversation drifting across other parts of the waiting room. Betty Sue picked up a magazine off the table beside her as Kelly scrolled through notifications on her phone. Jean and Hannah watched a couple enter with their son, who gingerly held a bag of frozen peas around his wrist. Through it all, Carla's gaze never left the rear door leading back into the emergency department.

When a nurse finally approached, she was on her feet. "How is she?"

"They're bringing her back in, so two of you can come with me. I'm sorry, but that's all we allow back there."

Carla met her mother's gaze and sighed. Betty Sue stood up, but addressed Jean instead. "I think she'd prefer you being with her," she croaked out, glancing at her daughter. "Am I right?"

Carla nodded, and Jean rose and took her hand. "C'mon, honey. We'll go find Nonna."

"Tell her I love her," Betty Sue called after her, wondering if Carla would rebuke her. She watched them follow the nurse as the door to the back swung closed. "I'm a terrible mother, aren't I?" She collapsed back in her seat as Hannah crossed the aisle to sit on her other side.

"No, you're not," Hannah said. "You gave up your spot in there because you knew you couldn't give Carla the support she needs tonight. I'd say you displayed a little empathy."

"She's right," Kelly added. "Carla's scared, and Jean's the best person to be with her. Hannah can take you back to see her when they come out."

Betty Sue patted the young blonde's hand. "You've taken such good care of my mother all these years – and me? I'm a screw up as a mother *and* a daughter."

"Enough with the drama," Kelly chimed in. "You're here now, okay? Save the therapy session for another day." Betty Sue sat like a chastised schoolgirl as Kelly anticipated major counseling sessions in the days to come.

———

Behind the doors, Carla stopped short in the doorway to her grandmother's room. "Oh my God; what's happened to her?" Elena's hands were wrapped in protective mitts as her arms twitched impulsively.

"You okay?" Jean gave her a reassuring hug.

"The doctor will be in shortly to talk to you," the nurse explained. "I'm sure she can answer all of your questions."

"Is it okay to touch her?" Carla asked.

"Absolutely. I'll be back in a couple of minutes to check her vitals again."

The monitor beside the bed beeped regularly as Carla approached the bed. "I can't even hold her hand with them all wrapped up."

"Tell you what," Jean said, "Why not sit right here, and you can stroke her hair – she always liked it when you brushed her hair at home."

Carla sat on the edge of the chair and tentatively reached out to touch her grandmother's head. "I'm here, Nonna. It's Carla." Tears spilled from her eyes as her grandmother's arms continued twitching. "I don't know if you can hear me...but I love you." She swallowed hard, wiping her face with her free hand. "Please don't...leave me yet."

Jean stood beside the chair and placed her hand on Carla's shoulder. "She knows you love her, honey. No matter what happens, she knows."

A young doctor entered the room, her thick black hair pulled back in a loose ponytail. "I'm Doctor Groner," she said, pushing her eyeglasses up the bridge of her nose before extending her hand. "And you're Carla?"

"Hmm-mm. Her granddaughter."

"And you're Carla's mom, I presume?"

"No. Jean McBride – a lifelong neighbor and friend. Elena's daughter Betty Sue is out in the waiting room; she thought Carla might prefer having me here."

"Why are her hands all wrapped up?" Carla asked. "And what's with all the twitching?"

Dr. Groner pulled up the other chair to sit at the foot of the bed.

"The arm movements are due to her stroke; they're neurological impulses right now – kind of like her brain is backfiring. She has no control over any of them, so the covering is protection in case she hits herself or the bed frame."

Carla winced as Elena's twitching continued. "Is she gonna be okay?"

Dr. Groner met Carla's gaze, her voice softening. "Carla, your grandmother had a massive stroke, and the bleeding in her brain is causing extensive damage. I'm so sorry."

Carla's eyes filled with tears as understanding settled in. "She's... gonna die?"

Jean, with tears in her eyes, squeezed Carla's shoulders as the doctor nodded slightly.

"I wish I had better news."

Carla's head dropped onto Elena's shoulder.

Jean rubbed her back and let her cry. "Is she in any pain?"

Dr. Groner shook her head. "I don't believe the brain is registering pain at this point, but we'll keep her comfortable just in case."

"Can...she...hear me?" Carla sobbed.

"It's a good idea to assume she can," Dr. Groner said calmly. "You can tell her what you need to while Jean goes out to fetch your mom. She needs to be here as well."

Jean leaned down and kissed Carla's head as she reached out to gently touch Elena's shoulder. "You stay and talk to Nonna and I'll bring your mom back." She met the doctor's gaze as she passed by. "I'll be right back. Betty Sue might have questions as well."

"I'll stick around. I need to check her vitals anyway."

Jean left the sounds of Elena's monitors and Carla's sobs behind her, stepping into the bustling hall of activity as she made her way to the waiting room. She met Hannah's gaze, conveying Elena's status with a sad shake of her head.

Betty Sue slumped with her elbows on the arms of her chair, her head resting in her hands, but she looked up when she saw Jean's feet in front of her.

"How is she?"

Jean reached for one of her friend's hands. "I'm so sorry, but she's not going to make it. You need to come with me."

"Why is everyone leaving me?" Betty Sue wailed. "Sean's in jail...and now she's gonna die on me!"

"Honey, you need to get a grip," Kelly said firmly. "I know you're dealing with a lot, but you're going in there, because your mom and daughter both need you."

"Not true," Betty Sue replied, turning to Hannah. "My daughter *hates* me."

Hannah placed her hand on Betty Sue's shoulder. "Look, you have to focus on Elena. She's been a special lady to all of us, so please go back and tell her how much we all love her, okay?"

"I...can do that." Betty Sue stood up. "Let's go," her voice faltered, but with Jean's support, she walked with resolve through the door. Her confidence wavered amidst a cacophony of beeps, bells, and bustling nurses.

"You've got this," Jean encouraged, leading her into Elena's room.

Betty Sue gasped when she saw her mother all bandaged up, and she rushed to the bedside across from Carla and leaned on the railing with one hand while patting Elena's shoulder with the other. "Oh,

Mother, I am so sorry...for everything...I'm such a bad daughter. Please don't leave me! I need to make it up to you!"

Carla sat quietly through her mother's gushing speech. "Very touching." Sarcasm slipped easily from her tear-stained face. "This is Dr. Groner, by the way, if you have any questions."

"I'm so sorry, doctor...where are my *manners* tonight?"

Jean stepped toward the door. *Southern drawl is back – not only when you're scared, but also when you need to impress someone.* "I'll let you both talk to the doctor. I'll be out with Hannah and Kelly."

Carla nodded as Jean slipped out, turning her attention once again to the frail, wrinkled face while the doctor explained everything to her mother. "There are several options at this point," Dr. Groner continued, glancing at Carla to include her in the conversation. "Why don't we step outside for a moment to chat?"

She led them to a relatively quiet spot in the hallway. "I'm sorry to say there's nothing we can do at this point except make her comfortable."

"You can't save her?" Betty Sue asked, grabbing the doctor's hand. "Maybe another doctor – or a hospital in Boston?"

"She's already gone," Carla said. "At least the woman she was. And there's no way she'd wanna be all hooked up to machines like she is."

"That was my next question," Dr. Groner replied. "Do you know if she has an advanced directive – explaining her wishes in this kind of situation?"

Carla nodded. "There's one on file in her records. From years back – she was adamant about not being kept alive like this."

"I'll have the nurse locate it. There's no guarantee she'll make it through the night, but if she does, there's a choice to be made. We'd bring in hospice – they can either move her home or to our hospice center next door, where they'd keep her comfortable. I know it's not an easy decision."

"I think the hospice center would be perfect," Betty Sue replied. "They'd have all the—"

"No." Carla faced her mother. "She's not gonna be shipped off someplace to die alone. And your opinion doesn't count for anything here." She turned to the doctor. "My grandmother also signed papers giving me power of attorney to make decisions if anything happened to her."

"You?"

Carla glared at her mother. "Why would it be anyone else? I've been taking care of her all these years." She turned toward Dr. Groner. "It's non-negotiable. She's coming *home*."

"I understand your position," Dr. Groner said. "But I do need to point out that in-home hospice doesn't include twenty four hour nursing care. I can recommend a few hospice nurses who provide it – but it's expensive, and rarely covered by insurance."

Carla sighed, deflated by the idea that cost might be an issue in granting her grandmother's wishes.

"Make whatever arrangements are needed for in-home care, and I'll take care of it," Betty Sue said quietly.

"I don't want your money," Carla hissed.

"For God's sake, Carla, I'm not giving you the money; I'm paying a bill you can't possibly cover so you can have her at home as you wish. I know we have lots to fight over, but please...let me do this one thing at least."

Carla swallowed hard, hating to accept the offer, but knowing she had no choice. "Fine."

"Okay, then," Dr. Groner said. "I'll start the process right away, and we can move Elena back home tomorrow. I know a semi-retired hospice nurse who specializes in short term end-of-life assignments. I'll have her contact you. And again, I'm so sorry the news isn't more positive."

Carla watched her walk away before meeting her mother's gaze. "Thank you," she uttered quietly, and not waiting for a reply, she turned and headed back into her grandmother's room.

# CHAPTER THREE

Carla was relieved when Jean and Hannah arrived before Elena was brought home. She finished moving the television into her grandmother's room shortly before they knocked and walked in. "In the bedroom," she called out as she heard their voices.

They joined her there, and Jean nodded approval at the television. "We may never know if she can actually hear them, but I think it brings peace to all of us to know her favorite game shows will be on in the background."

"The hospice nurse said the same thing this morning when she came to check the house. She'll be back shortly to help get Nonna settled."

As they headed back down the hall, Jean wrapped her arm around Carla. "And how are *you* doing? Did you sleep at all?"

"A little. I'm kinda numb, actually. Everything happened so fast. And this morning was crazy as I talked to the hospital, called Mr. Winston about the legal stuff, and then had the nurse show up."

"You can rest a bit once your Gram is back," Hannah said. "I'm so glad you're bringing her home. She lived her whole life here."

Carla's eyes welled up. "Yeah...she deserves to take her last breath here, too." She sank down on the couch. "I gotta admit; I hope it's not too long. It's gonna be weird just sitting here waiting for her to die."

"I'm sure the hospice nurse will help you along the way," Jean said. "So...where's your mother?"

"I told her I'd call when Nonna arrives. I didn't want her here right away; is that wrong?"

"Not at all. You've earned some time alone with your grandmother. I'll call her when you're in helping to get Elena settled."

A car door slammed outside, and Carla got up to answer the door. "That'll be the hospice nurse. She's really nice." She greeted the middle-aged woman and invited her in. "This is my second family – Jean McBride, and Hannah, my best friend. And this is Trisha Patterson, the hospice nurse."

"So nice to meet you both," Trisha said, extending her hand. "Carla's told me how special you both are. And Hannah, you've been her caregiver during the day?"

"Over two years now. It's gonna be hard to see her go."

"At least she'll be free of the dementia," Jean offered. "I'm glad she still knew all of us."

"That's true," Trisha said gently, "But it doesn't make the goodbye any easier. Please know I'm here for all of you, not just Elena. Carla, is...your mother here, or coming later?"

"Jean's gonna call her. I wanted to welcome Nonna home without—"

"You don't have to justify or explain your choices," Trisha assured. "Why don't we go and get the bed all set? The ambulance should be on its way."

Carla led Trisha down the hall while Jean and Hannah kept watch for Elena's arrival. Within fifteen minutes, Hannah called down the hall. "Ambulance is coming!"

Carla came rushing out of the room behind Trisha, whose pace was relaxed. "There's no need to rush, my dear," Trisha said, taking Carla's hand as they reached the living room. "The next few days are all about slowing down...letting nature take its own course. Do you think you can do that?"

"I...have no idea. I've been rushing my whole life."

"Then consider this time a present from your Nonna. Even if she can't interact with you, she's asking you to simply be with her – for as long as she has. What a special gift that is, don't you think?"

Carla nodded as Jean opened the door for the paramedics, and smiled as her grandmother was wheeled in. "Nonna..." she whispered, gently kissing her grandmother's forehead. *Welcome home...one last time.* "No bandages?"

"They're not needed now that she's medicated," Trisha explained. "She'll be much more comfortable this way." Turning to the paramedics, she continued. "Her room is this way. I'll take you back."

Hannah reached for Carla's hand as Trisha led them down the hall. "You okay?"

Her friend nodded, blinking back tears. "She's right, though. Even though it's for the best, this isn't gonna be easy..."

"Why don't you two sit while they get your Nonna settled," Jean said. "I'm gonna go pick up your mom so she doesn't have to drive, and she can stay with me tonight."

"Thanks. I wasn't sure where I was gonna put her. I gave my old room to Trisha, and the spare room is full of junk."

"You let me handle your Mom, and tell me if you need some respite from her. I can drag her butt across the street at any time. I won't be long."

———

Once the paramedics left, Trisha joined Carla in the bedroom to wait for Betty Sue's arrival. Hannah offered the hospice nurse her seat. "Can I make either of you some coffee or tea?"

"I would love a cup of tea," Trisha said.

"Anything in it?"

"I often put a touch of lemon, but plain is fine – thank you."

Hannah turned to Carla. "Coffee?"

"Stupid question."

"Iced with a touch of milk – comin' right up," Hannah said, heading for the kitchen.

"She's a good friend," Trisha said. "She knows how you drink your coffee."

"She's more like a sister. We've grown up together. She spent a lot of time here after school; her mom taught at the high school and usually got home closer to dinner time."

"And she's been Nonna's caregiver during the day?"

"No one besides me knows her better – except maybe her mom."

Trisha noticed the quilt folded on the back of Carla's chair. "Is that another homemade quilt behind you? I know you told me your grandmother made the one covering her, but I really like those colors."

Carla gently fingered the edge of the quilt by her shoulder. "She made this one for me when I was little – all the colors of the sea, she said. I moved it in here this morning before you came."

"I'm sure you'll appreciate having something Nonna made while you spend time in here."

Carla gazed at the patchwork quilt on the bed, watching her grandmother's chest rise and fall underneath it. "She sewed that one as a wedding gift to my grandfather; said it was the one thing she'd grab aside from me if we ever had a fire."

"I imagine both quilts have a special place in your heart right now."

"There are four scattered around the house. When I was little, I'd curl up next to her to read, and she'd point to the different squares and tell me stories about the fabrics, and what she cut up to make all the patches."

"All the little bits of love and warmth you've shared over the years?"

"In so many ways," Carla replied. "Right up until her dementia started, she'd sit out on the back porch in her rocking chair, all nice and toasty in her quilt."

"I spotted an old rocking chair out front when I arrived; it's such a lovely view of the harbor."

"She liked the back porch more; she could watch the neighborhood fishermen coming in at the end of the day." Carla smiled, her mind flooded with countless memories of the handmade treasures as Elena's breath filled the silence.

"Why does she sound so weird?" Carla asked.

"Some people call it the death rattle," Trisha replied, "and it can be a little scary to hear. As the body starts to shut down, it's not able to clear the mucus and saliva we normally produce, so it starts to rattle as it settles in the lungs. She may cough from time to time, or continue to breathe weird. It's all part of the process." She paused a moment before continuing. "One question I have for you: was your grandmother a religious woman? I didn't know if you'd want me to call a priest or minister to stop by."

"A priest anointed her in the hospital; I assume it counts?"

Trisha laughed. "Absolutely. And how about you? Anyone you'd like me to contact?"

"Nope, I'm good. Went to Mass with Nonna when I was little, but I didn't get anything out of it." Carla watched Elena's chest rise and fall in shallow breaths. "So how many people have you...ya know—"

"Been with as they died? I'm not sure I could give you an exact number, but probably several dozen over the years."

"Jeez...isn't it hard?"

"Isn't what hard?" Hannah asked, returning with requested drinks.

"Carla was asking if it's been hard to watch so many people die over the years," Trisha said, taking the teacup and saucer. "I feel humbled and somewhat privileged to be able to help them cross over to their next journey."

"You must be a special kind of person," Carla replied. "I'm sort of dreading this. I don't know what to expect."

"What you're feeling is normal," Trisha explained. "Don't be afraid of any of your emotions; they can be overwhelming at times and hit like a wave out of the blue, but there's no wrong way to feel."

Carla's eyes filled with tears as she reached over to hold Elena's hand. "How am I gonna live without the one who's taken care of me since I was little?"

"It's okay to be uncertain," Trisha said. "And I'm not here only for Elena. Part of what I do is to help family members go through the process as well. I suspect I may need to help both you and your mother."

Carla sighed heavily, gently stroking the frail hand in hers with her thumb. "I'll be honest. I don't know if I'm gonna be able to handle her being here – I don't need her drama when I'm trying to say goodbye."

"I understand," Trisha replied. "And if it helps, I've worked with many families who have far more strife than what's between you and your mother. It's important for all of you to be honest. I can help mediate when needed."

"You might have your hands full," Hannah offered. "There's a whole lot of hurt between Carla and her mom."

The sound of voices wafted down the hall. "And I guess it's time for you to meet Betty Sue first hand. I'll bring her back." Patting Carla on the shoulder, she added, "Just be you. For Nonna."

Carla was expecting her mom's exuberant Southern Belle persona she used when meeting strangers, but Betty Sue entered the room like a scared child, reluctant to look at her mother lying in bed.

"You must be Betty Sue," Trisha said warmly, getting up to shake her hand and offer her chair as she pulled up the folding chair beside her. "I'm Trisha Patterson, the hospice nurse, and I'll be here to help you both through the next few days."

Betty Sue held onto her hand as she perched on the side of her chair. "It's so nice of you to come and move right in," she said. "I didn't know that was even an option."

"Most of the time hospice workers will visit regularly, but some of us are available for short term exclusive care. It's so much easier on the family to only have one or two people to deal with. Do you have any questions for me? I was talking to Carla before you arrived, explaining your mother's raspy breathing."

"I...know about that," Betty Sue whispered. "My husband Kenneth – God rest his soul – had a sister die of cancer, and she sounded like that the last time we visited." She finally found courage to glance at her mother's face. "She looks so ashen."

"It's almost like she's dying," Carla replied sarcastically. "You don't have to be here, you know. I'm used to dealing with Nonna on my own."

Betty Sue's eyes filled with tears. "Can we not fight? It's hard enough just being here; I don't think I can handle your attitude on top of it."

"My *attitude?* Really?"

Trisha intervened. "Ladies, I realize how much anger and hurt there's been between you over the years, and it's normal to express your emotions – necessary, even. But I'd like to suggest some ground rules for when you're in this room with Elena, if that's okay."

"Whatever." Carla avoided eye contact with either of them, focusing on Elena as she stroked her hand.

"What...kind of rules?" Betty Sue asked.

"I'd like this room to be as peaceful as we can make it. Elena loves both of you, and I know you both love her in your own ways. So, while you're in here, I'm suggesting each of you focus on Elena, and allow the other to be authentic in saying goodbye without judgment – even if it means not talking to each other. Out in the living room or kitchen, you'll have the freedom to interact and express yourselves. Do you think you can both try that?"

"I'm sure we can manage that," Betty Sue replied. "Can't we, Carla?"

"Might be easier if we took turns being in here."

"That was my next suggestion, actually. I think you both have things to say to Elena that you'd feel uncomfortable saying with the other present – am I right?"

Carla found Trisha's gentle manner soothing. "Without a doubt." Betty Sue nodded quietly.

"Carla, why don't you give your mom and I a few minutes with your nonna? I know you said you needed to call the attorney to set up a meeting here at the house?"

"Yeah, I can go do that." Carla leaned over and kissed her grandmother's forehead. "I'll be right back, Nonna. I love you."

As she stood up, Trisha smiled reassuringly. "And have a little something to eat, okay? You need to take care of yourself as well."

"I will."

Carla grabbed her coffee mug and slipped out, closing the door halfway. Betty Sue watched her go, her stomach churning. "I'm...not sure how to do this," she admitted. "I haven't exactly been close to either of them all these years."

Trisha reached out to rest her hand on Betty Sue's shoulder. "I imagine you must be feeling a lot of emotions all at once. Nervousness, some sadness, and maybe a little guilt?"

Betty Sue's eyes filled with tears as Trisha identified that last emotion. "I haven't been a very good daughter – and even a worse mother. And now I'll never get a chance to make it right."

"Do you believe in God?" Trisha asked.

"Kenneth and I went to church every Sunday when he was alive. I... can't say I've continued since he passed..."

"But you must believe he went to a better place?"

"Oh, without a doubt. My dear Kenneth was the finest person I've ever known. And I know he went straight to heaven."

"Do you still talk to him?"

"All the time," Betty Sue said. "He's always watching over me – well, maybe not when I was with Sean, but certainly before then."

"And Sean is—"

"He *was* my boyfriend...or so I thought. Turns out he only wanted my money."

"I'm sorry to hear that. Sounds like you're dealing with a lot of loss."

"I get angry with myself because I loved him– he was nothing like my Kenneth."

"But he still made you feel special, didn't he?"

Betty Sue started sobbing. "I...felt...beautiful again. But he's a bad, bad man." She gulped hard as the anger returned.

"It's okay to let it out," Trisha said, handing her the tissue box.

"I'm sorry for carrying on like this," Betty Sue mumbled. "You're supposed to be here for mother, not me."

"That's not true," Trisha replied. "I'm here for all of you. You'll grieve in your way, and you have other stuff in your life thrown into the mix. Everything you're feeling about Sean right now is part of you, and you can't simply turn those emotions off as you say goodbye to your mother."

"You're such a wise woman. I'm...glad you're here."

"Me, too. I suspect Elena guided me here. She knew you and Carla would have trouble going through this without help."

"Mother stashed her slippers in the refrigerator; decision making wasn't exactly her strong suit."

"That may be true since her dementia hit, but what about years ago? Wasn't she a strong and practical woman?"

"She was the strongest woman I ever knew," Betty Sue said.

"Well, I believe that people with dementia leave us twice. The first time is long and slow and painful to watch, but I believe their spirit is exactly as you remember it. This last step, when the body finally slips away, simply allows the spirit to be released as free and whole as it ever was."

For a moment only Elena's breathing was heard. "I don't think I've ever heard death described so beautifully," Betty Sue murmured. "Thank you for that − truly."

"You're welcome. And doesn't that image make it easier to consider your mom loves you as much as she ever did, and will still be watching over you, wanting you to be happy again?"

Betty Sue finally turned her attention to her mother, reaching out tenuously to take her hand. "That would be nice, but I'm not sure I deserve it. Mother...I never should have left you and Carla...it was so wrong of me, and I'm really sorry."

Carla stood in the doorway, hearing her mother express remorse for the first time. She blinked back her own tears as she avoided her mother's gaze. "I...got in touch with Mr. Winston. He said we can meet... after...you know."

"After your grandmother passes," Trisha replied. "I know it's hard to actually say the word death, but it gets easier if you realize it's part of life."

*If you say so. All I know is I don't know how to do this. Why couldn't death come and take my mother, and leave Nonna and I alone? And if I'm wrong to feel that way, then so be it.*

# CHAPTER FOUR

Carla finally dozed off sometime after midnight, curled up in the recliner next to Elena's bed. Betty Sue had gone home with Jean and Hannah, and Trisha had retreated to the spare room to catch a few hours of sleep. For hours, Carla had wrapped herself up in her quilt and studied the varied blue and green strips sewn together. She noticed the tiny stitches her grandmother had done by hand.

She didn't know if Elena could hear her, but she talked to her anyway. "God, I used to drag this thing to the beach in the summer. Hannah and I would stretch out in the sun and talk about mermaids and pirates and cute boys all day. Remember how you'd yell at me to get it in the wash right away when I got home so the colors wouldn't fade?" *It's definitely faded some, but it was made to last. Your quilts will probably last long after both of us are gone.*

Eventually Carla got tired and tried to sleep, but all she could hear was the quiet death rattle. She finally put on the television and found an old movie she and Nonna liked, keeping the volume quiet enough not to wake Trisha, but loud enough to hear over Elena's breathing.

She awoke with a start early the next morning as Trisha tip toed into the room. "I'm sorry I woke you; I was trying to be quiet."

"It's okay," Carla yawned. She looked out to see the promise of dawn in the eastern sky. "How is she?"

She watched as Trisha examined her grandmother. "Exactly as she should be." She came around the bed and sat down next to Carla, speaking softly. "Her breathing and heart rate are slowing down and becoming more irregular. She may stop breathing occasionally for short periods, and then you might hear a deeper breath. At some point later today, there will be a final breath – and then peace."

Carla wrapped the quilt tighter. "I'm gonna miss her so much."

"I heard you talking to her last night as I drifted off to sleep. I'm sure it helped."

"It did. I doubt she could hear me, but I told her all my favorite memories of our life together, and wished her nothing but a safe journey to wherever it is she's going." Tears welled up again. "And now I'm crying again, damn it."

"People who grieve deeply are people who have loved deeply, and it's clear you two shared a profound love. Why don't you let me sit with her a bit and you can go grab a few hours of sleep?"

Carl shook her head. "I don't think I could sleep."

Trisha nodded with understanding. "Can I at least bring you some coffee?"

"That'd be appreciated."

"I'll be right back."

As Trisha made her way around the bed, Carla caught her eye and smiled. "I'm glad you're here. I don't think I could do this alone."

"I am, too. I know it wasn't easy allowing your mom to cover the finances, but I think it was a positive step for both of you."

Carla shrugged. "I'm sure it's all out of guilt."

"Deep seated guilt can also be a sign of deep love – something to keep in mind."

*Not sure I buy that theory...but I have to admit I'm glad her guilty conscience paid for having Nonna home. Now if I can get through the day without biting her head off, I'll take it as a win.*

An incoming text interrupted her thoughts. *Paul.* She couldn't help but smile that he'd taken the time to check in on her. He'd only been in town a few months, but the first time he came into the Even Keel for a drink they clicked, and she'd been seeing him ever since. *I'm doing okay. Final goodbyes most likely today. Thanks for checking in.* She texted back, grateful for this new guy in her life who didn't care about Carla's past reputation.

"Well, something put a smile on your face." Trisha delivered a mug of coffee before sitting down across the bed.

Carla blushed. "His name is Paul. He wanted to know how I was doing."

"Boyfriend?"

"I...guess he is," Carla replied.

"You guess?" Trisha chuckled. "How do you not know something like that?"

"I've never really *had* a boyfriend. Most guys in town saw me as the girl to hook up with, not one to date or take home to mom."

"And Paul's different?"

Carla's stomach fluttered a bit at the realization. "He is. He came into town a few months ago and I served him a drink one night. He kept coming back in and sitting at the bar, and we'd talk and laugh, and then one night he asked me out. And for the first time I went on a date without sleeping with the guy afterwards."

"Must have been a special date."

"Kinda weird, actually. We walked on the beach and talked – he was fascinated with the signs on Long Beach keeping people away from the Piping Plover nests."

"Haven't they all migrated by now?"

"Yeah, but some of the signs are still up. He wanted to know all about them – why they're endangered, how many are nesting here each summer, and whether it's the same pairs that come back every year. He thought it was neat these little birds mated for life, and the community was working so hard to keep their little families alive."

"Sounds like someone to keep around."

"I hope so. Sometimes I'm scared he's stringing me along until he gets what all the others have had."

"If you've been seeing him three months without any kind of pressure, I'd say he's not like the other guys."

"I guess we'll see."

Trisha met her gaze. "Maybe *you've* changed as well. Feeling surer of yourself?"

"Never thought of it that way," Carla replied, considering the idea. "Maybe I am growing a little." Elena startled her with a deep rattling breath. "Is she okay?"

"She stopped breathing for a few seconds. It's totally normal."

"Is she in any pain?"

"She doesn't appear to be, and if I see any signs I can give a small dose of morphine. One thing I'd like you and your mother to do this morning is to call anyone else you know who would want to say good bye. Being at home allows you some freedom in having visitors stop by to show support."

"Can I grab a quick shower first? If you think there's time."

"If anything changes, I'll bang on the bathroom door, okay?"

Carla left the quilt on the back of the chair and kissed Elena. "I'll be right back, Nonna. Give me a few minutes and then I'll sit with you for as long as you need me."

———

Later that day, with several friends in the room, Carla held her grandmother's hand as she took her last breath. "Go in peace, Nonna," she whispered, kissing her forehead with tears in her eyes. "I'll miss you so much."

Betty Sue burst into tears as she got up to leave the room. "I can't do this!"

Kelly started to follow her, but Trisha put her hand up. "I'll go. All of you can take your time saying goodbye."

She found Betty Sue rocking back and forth on the couch, clutching a pillow. When she sat down, Betty Sue's sobs got louder. "I... never...got to...make it right..."

Trisha rubbed her back and spoke calmly. "That's not entirely true. You made it possible for me to be here for your mom and for Carla."

"I should have...been here more. And been...nicer."

"I know one way you could make amends to her – it won't be easy, but I know it's what she would have wanted."

Betty Sue sat up straighter and wiped her eyes. "Tell me. I'll do anything."

Trisha met her gaze. "Make things right with your daughter."

"But...you don't understand...Carla hates me. She'll never forgive me."

"Like I said, it won't be easy. Carla is angry and hurt – and has every right to be – but inside she still wants family. And the only family she's known just left her."

"I'm telling you, she'll never come around."

"She needs to see *you* making the effort. If not, then I suspect you'll be right and she'll move on without you."

"But I don't know *how* to be alone!" Betty Sue's next round of tears began again as Kelly, Terri, and Peg joined them in time to hear her, and Peg's response was less gentle than the hospice nurse.

"For God's sake, Betty Sue, you're *not* alone! You have friends who love you – despite yourself—and a daughter who might surprise you if you gave her a chance."

Trisha stood up to make room for the others. "I'll leave you to chat so I can take of things that need to be done. Betty Sue, I'd be happy to sit with you if you have any final goodbyes for your mom. And if not, I do hope you find peace through all of this."

"Can I wait a couple more minutes?"

"Absolutely. You can come back when the others are done saying goodbye. Okay?"

Betty Sue nodded as Kelly sat down next to her to talk. "You're stronger than you think you are. You just have to learn it can't always be about you. Everyone here is dealing with their own emotions after losing Elena – but none more than your daughter."

Terri nodded. "She's right. Carla has to be feeling really alone."

Betty Sue sighed. "Do you really think there's a chance for us to reconcile?"

"I don't know," Kelly replied. "It takes two. But if you don't at least try, you're gonna someday die a lonely and bitter old woman."

"I can't bear the idea of being alone, but I'm scared she'd never forgive me for leaving her all those years."

"I think you have to start by actually apologizing," Peg said.

Terri nodded. "But only if you really mean it – Carla can see through bullshit better than most."

"But she doesn't even want me here – how will she ever let me explain?"

"You have to respect her space right now," Kelly said. "She's grieving the loss of the person she loves most in this world – and the one who loved her the most. You can't push your way in to her life; you have to be patient and persistent."

Voices wafted down the hall as Jean, Hannah, Paul, and Carla appeared.

"Trisha said you could go in," Jean said as the others went into the kitchen. "Then you can come stay with Hannah and me tonight. Carla wants a little time alone after we all leave."

"Come on," Kelly said, as Jean sat on the far end of the couch. "I'll go with you if you'd like." She took her friend's hand and led her down the hall to say goodbye.

# CHAPTER FIVE

Carla walked Paul outside as Jean and Hannah cleaned up the kitchen.

He leaned against his truck and opened his arms, inviting her in for a hug. She buried her face in his flannel, breathing in the smell of him. Even though he'd only come into her life several months earlier, she felt safe with him.

"You okay?" he whispered. She nodded, still sniffling. "I can hang around – at least until..."

"They take her away?" She finished his sentence, leaning back to look up into his eyes. "It's okay; Trisha will be here, and she'll stay a bit."

He gently brushed her curls back behind her ear. "If you need me later, just call. I hate the idea of you being all alone tonight."

Carla actually smiled. "You trying to proposition me in my grieving state?"

Paul laughed out loud and pulled her in closer. "Much as I love the idea of finally spending a night with you, tonight's not the time for that. Besides, I don't want you all teary eyed and snotty for our first time together."

Carla allowed the anticipation of being with Paul to mingle with the emptiness of losing Elena. "I don't know what I'd do without you right now," she mumbled into his shirt.

"Well, that's not something you have to worry about." Paul rested his chin on top of her head and held her, caring more and more about this sarcastic, down-to-earth woman who caught his eye the first time he walked into the Even Keel. He'd lost his mom a year back, and after watching his dad turn to alcohol for solace, he packed his belongings into his old truck and left Maine to find a new life in Gloucester.

"I better let you get back inside," he said. "And I'm really glad you let me come over to meet her a few times. I'll miss her laugh." Paul cupped her face gently with his hands and kissed her. "Can I see you tomorrow after work?"

"I'd like that. It'll be a busy day. We have to go to the funeral home in the morning and then meet with the lawyer in the afternoon."

"Can't that wait until after the funeral?"

"The lawyer has all her paperwork, and I'd rather get everything done as soon as possible. Jean and Hannah said they'd bring my mom over in the morning, and then stay and have lunch ready before the meeting with Mr. Winston."

"You gonna be okay at the funeral home with just your mom?"

"Trisha's coming along for that, and then she'll leave from there. Jean will stay for the other meeting at home; it'll be easier with her there."

"You do realize at some point you're gonna have to be alone with your mom?"

Carla sighed. "Yeah...and it scares the hell out of me." She kissed Paul one more time and pulled herself out of his embrace as tears welled up in her eyes. "But first, I have to go in and say goodbye to Nonna one last time. I'll see you tomorrow." She turned and paused when she reached the back door, looking back to wave as he got into his truck. *Please help me through this, Nonna. And if you can, please have Paul stick around. He might be exactly what I need to learn how to live without you.*

———

Later that afternoon, across the street, Jean took a pan of lasagna out of the oven after stirring a pot of chili on the stove. *These should feed both Carla and Betty Sue for a few days.* The latter had gone to the guest room to nap a while, so she enjoyed a quiet cup of coffee at the table and recalled countless memories with Elena over the years.

Hannah joined her with an empty travel mug in her hand. "Hmm... smells good in here. For Carla, no doubt?"

"Yeah; I figure we could order take out; it's been a long day, and the next few days will be the same. Anything you might like?"

Hannah refilled her container with iced water. "Sorry, but I'm bailing on both of you. Won't Kim be home soon? She can eat with you."

"She's working late; some concert at the castle."

"I hope it's not another organ recital by that dorky professor. He's been asking Kim out for months, and I'm so afraid she's gonna do something stupid and say yes."

"You have a problem with your sister dating again? I think after three years you'd be happy to see her find someone else."

"Not him, though! She belongs with Bill, and everyone knows it but her!"

Jean got up and carried her empty mug to the sink, rinsing it out before placing it in the strainer. "Kim said she'd never date a fisherman again – not after losing Anthony. I like Bill just as much as you do, but he's already got a major strike against him." She tasted the chili, and finding it satisfactory, turned the burner off. "So where are you off to?"

"Over to JJ's. Making progress on his GED prep. He's so smart, Mom."

"Tell him I said hi. And I'm glad he's taking this step; it will help."

"He's really motivated; he has big dreams, and knows he needs the education to achieve them."

"Good for him," Jean replied. "And give Arlene my love if she's home. I'll be seeing Jim tomorrow about all the legal stuff, but won't see her until the wake and funeral."

"Will do," Hannah said, giving her mom a quick hug. "I won't be late. Love you!"

———

It was a short drive through town to get to the Winston's home by the cemetery. Hannah parked on the street and rang the front doorbell, and Arlene answered almost immediately. "Hannah! How nice to see you again! Come in."

"Hi, Mrs. Winston; nice to see you, too. I hope it's not inconvenient."

"Not at all. James is dining at the club with a colleague, and JJ insisted on buying pizza so I didn't have to cook. He's got all his stuff laid out on the table downstairs."

As they passed through the living room, Hannah's attention was drawn to Arlene's latest knitting project next to her chair. "I love the blue and orange together! Another blanket?"

Arlene stopped, always excited when someone talked about her favorite hobby. "You have to feel how soft this yarn is," she said. "I think I'll be keeping this one."

Hannah ran her hand over the soft complementary colors. "Wow, that's gonna be wonderful to curl up in once it's gets cold." She admired other afghans around the room.

"See? I told ya!" JJ stood in the doorway leaning against the jam. "She could sell this stuff and make money, but she doesn't believe she's got talent."

"It's not proper to brag about oneself," Arlene replied as she placed the blanket back on her chair. "We're supposed to be humble."

"But aren't you supposed to let your light shine and all that stuff?" JJ grinned at his mom, and then met Hannah's gaze with a wider smile.

*God, that smile. I'll never get tired of it. And I love seeing him and his mom getting closer again.*

"Pizza arrived just before you did," JJ said. "I invited Mom to join us to eat, but she said she'd prefer a quick slice before watching a chick flick on her own."

"It's not a chick flick!" Arlene's cheeks flushed as she passed her son. "It's a story about the power of love on the Christian station. Your father would never approve of a chick flick."

"Whatever you say, Mom," JJ teased as he passed Hannah a plate. "But Dad might not be home for a couple of hours, and I bet it's not the only movie on television tonight – just sayin'." He opened the pizza box, and closed his eyes as scents of onions, peppers, and cheese mingled together in the air. "Thank you, God, for pizza."

"Was that grace?" Hannah asked with a sheepish grin.

"Absolutely. Obviously a gift to the world."

Arlene handed them each a napkin. "Enough of that. Take your food and heathen attitude downstairs and let me enjoy some peace."

Hannah chuckled at the banter as she followed JJ down to the family room. As they sat down at the table, she slid a couple of books back to make room for their plates. "I wonder how she'd feel if she knew you'd invited a true Pagan into your house – complete with tarot cards in her bag?"

"Shh..." JJ whispered with a grin. "Some things she might find hard to joke about – even if she does love having you come over."

"I promise I'll leave the tarot cards at home next time."

JJ laughed. "Well, there hasn't been any lightning bolt striking you down yet, so I think we're good. Pass me that book and I'll get it out of your way."

As their hands touched, Hannah felt a charge of energy shoot up her arm. *Zeus may not have struck me down with a lightning bolt, but you're sure zapping me with electricity, pal.*

Over the next couple of hours, Hannah was amazed at how smart JJ was, and how quickly he grasped new concepts. "Jeez, sometimes I think you know more than your tutor. You'll breeze through this test in no time."

"Ya think?" JJ closed his laptop. "I'm not as confident, I guess. All I know is I really want this; I'll never get my foot in the door with any reputable builder without it. Hey, it's still early. Wanna kick back and watch something?"

"Sure, I'd like that."

"And I don't know about you, but I need more pizza. Want another couple slices?"

"Maybe one more – and don't heat mine up. I really like cold pizza."

JJ grinned. "A girl after my own heart. Get comfy – be back in a sec."

She walked over to the other side of the room where a couch and recliner faced a modest size television, and was drawn to a pad of graph paper with sketches on the couch. It only took a moment or two before she realized what he was drawing. *Oh, my God; this is a tiny house design!* She and JJ had spent the day at a tiny house convention recently, and she was thrilled to see that he loved them as much as she did. He'd spent the day talking to each builder about the various specs, soaking in every detail of each house.

She looked up when JJ returned with the pizza. "Sorry; I couldn't help myself. This is an awesome design!"

"It's coming along," JJ replied, totally unfazed that she had taken a look without asking. He handed her a plate and plopped down next to her, clicking on the remote as he took a quick bite.

Hannah couldn't help but laugh. "And of course you watch HGTV. How appropriate."

"Hey, I'll put on anything you want. Aside from football, I don't really watch much else. Always getting new ideas to work with."

Hannah took a bite of pizza, moving the sketches to a small table next to the couch. "I don't wanna get any grease on those, but would love to see more when we're done. You keep talking about getting a job with one of the builders, but you could almost start your own business and work for yourself. You're certainly talented enough."

"I've actually thought about it, but it might not be that easy starting a business with a drug charge on my record. Ya know, for bank loans and stuff. Besides, there's way more to learn about the business end if I tried to do it myself."

"Maybe you should think about a business degree. To keep your options open."

JJ grinned. "Maybe I will. Would you tutor me through college?"

Hannah laughed. "Hell, no. I haven't even gone myself yet."

"So, what do *you* wanna do? I mean, aside from living in a tiny house – which will require a job to pay for it."

"Honestly? I'm not sure what I'm gonna do now that Elena's gone..."

"How are you doing? I know how close you two were."

"She was my adopted grandma; mine died when I was really young, and Elena was always there, right across the street. Carla and I would help her with baking and cooking, and she'd always welcome whoever came to the door. I remember she told me you could always add something to stretch a meal if an extra person showed up. She was probably the most hospitable person I ever knew."

"Sounds like those memories will stick with you; bet you learned a lot from her."

Hannah nodded, smiling as countless images of Elena flitted through her mind. "I'll miss her a lot, but I'm glad she died before the dementia got any worse."

"Yeah, from the little I've seen, that's a disease I wouldn't wish on anyone," JJ said, his tone softer. "I hope you know I'm here for you, if you ever wanna talk or need a hug."

"Thanks. I know I can count on you...and I can't wait to see what kind of great job you end up with."

"Which reminds me – you never answered the question. You must have *some* dream job tucked away inside."

"I do actually. I'm just not sure how well it would be received around here. Or how some people might judge me."

JJ leaned toward her, almost whispering. "If you're thinking about a career as a pole dancer, I for one believe you'd be amazing at it – and I promise I'd never tell my mother."

Hannah laughed out loud. "Oh, God. She'd ban you from seeing me and then tell my mother that she was a total failure in controlling her child." Hannah sat quietly for a moment before replying. "Come to think of it, she might do the exact same thing if I end up following my dream."

"Now I'm intrigued."

"What I'd really love to do," Hannah said, "Is to have my own tarot reading business online."

"I think you'd be great at that; you're so naturally intuitive. So, what's stopping you, girl?"

"Well, let's see," Hannah replied, counting on her fingers for each item. "There's self-doubt, fear of being judged, fear of making a fool out of myself, fear of no customers...how am I doing?"

"Impressive list, I must commend you. Bet you've given it all tons of thought."

"Yeah, mostly at two in the morning when I wake up and can't get back to sleep."

"Some wise woman told me that being awake with deep thoughts during the night is a sign from the universe that we have lessons to learn, and negative emotions need releasing in order to manifest something great."

Hannah whacked his arm. "Wise woman, my ass. I told you that when we were at the tiny house convention."

"Exactly my point. Don't give up on the dream before even giving it a shot. Worse that can happen is you fail – but you'll still learn the lesson you need before moving on to something else."

"Have you always been this smart? About life, I mean?"

JJ grinned. "I think maybe you bring out the best in me." He stretched out his arm and rested it on the back of the couch, reaching down with his thumb to stroke her hair. "I'm really glad we reconnected. I love every minute we spend together."

"Me, too." Hannah met his gaze as he leaned in and kissed her, closing her eyes as their lips met and Zeus finally delivered on that lightning bolt through her body.

# CHAPTER SIX

Carla woke up after a restless sleep in her grandmother's bed. Trisha had changed the sheets after Elena's body had been taken away, and Carla had spent the night curled up in her quilt, lulled to sleep by the familiar scent of the lotion she'd massaged lovingly onto Nonna's dry skin, only to wake up in the dark, listening for the rattling breath and being overwhelmed by an almost screaming stillness.

*Nonna, how am I gonna do this without you? I want your laugh back; I want the frustration of finding your slippers in the refrigerator, or your dirty dishes in the washing machine. You've been the one whose made me who I am — but I don't know who that is without you.* She let the tears flow in loud sobs that wracked her body, clinging tightly to the last scents that still mingled in the damp quilt.

An incoming text interrupted her grief, and fighting the desire to ignore it, Carla hit the button instead, welcoming a selfie of Paul at the Even Keel with her boss behind him. "Stopped by last night and Joey sends his love; says to take whatever time you need. We're both here for ya, Squirt. I'll check in later."

She couldn't help but smile. Her boss, Joey, had nicknamed her "Squirt" when she first started working there in high school, and now ten years later Paul had started using the name as well. *My second home.*

*Much as I've wanted to get out of this friggin' town, the Keel has been the most welcoming place I've known aside from here – it even brought Paul into my life.*

Glancing at the time, she groaned and sat up, collecting the pile of dirty tissues scattered on the bed and dumping them in the trash. "Ready or not, it's time to face the day. Nonna, I sure hope your spirit is sticking around awhile to help me through the next few days. Gotta get ready for the first meeting without you."

Trisha had spent the night, but stayed in her room to give Carla some needed privacy. She had slipped out earlier in the morning, leaving a note on the counter that she'd meet Carla and her mom at the funeral home before heading back to her own home in Ipswich.

Within an hour, the back door opened and Hannah's familiar voice called out. "Elen—I mean, Carla. It's Hannah." *I guess it'll take a while for all of us to realize we don't have to announce ourselves for Nonna's sake.* Glancing in the mirror at her black pants and top, she stood straight up and exhaled toward her reflection. *Well, this should be fun. Thank God the funeral home is only a few blocks away.*

She welcomed hugs from Hannah and Jean as her mother stood by the back door, still awkwardly holding a casserole dish. Carla noted the puffy eyes and assumed Betty Sue had done her own crying – probably on Jean's shoulder. "Morning, Mother."

"I'm all ready," Betty Sue replied. "I...hope you got a little sleep." She offered the meal, almost as a peace offering. "We – well, Jean – made you some food. There's lasagna and chili; they made me some as well."

Carla accepted the dish, her stomach growling a bit. She noticed the lasagna pan Jean had placed on the table, as well as a second plate of mini muffins. "You didn't have to do that, but thanks."

Hannah took the chili from her and stuffed a mini muffin in her hand. "She knew you'd forget to eat – and I heard that stomach rumble, so eat this quick on the way. We're gonna make a pot of soup and some salad so you'll have lunch ready when you get back."

"You two are the best," Betty Sue said. "And I'll have the whole gang over for brunch in a day or two to say thank you."

"I...guess we better get going." Carla wasn't sure if she dreaded the meeting or the drive alone with her mother more, but both loomed directly in front of her. "We'll be back."

Jean offered one more hug. "Nonna's right there whispering in your ear. You've got this." Turning to Betty Sue, she continued. "I'll stick around for the meeting with James, and then you can come stay with me as long as you need to afterwards."

Betty Sue grasped her hand. "I don't know how I would have gotten through last night without you." Reluctantly, she followed Carla out and slipped into the seat beside her. The radio played classic rock as Carla started the car. "Okay if I keep the music on?" The opening bars of AC/DC's "Highway to Hell" blasted as Betty Sue nodded. *Talk about the perfect song choice. And it's just long enough to get us there, I bet.*

Trisha was waiting at the funeral home, and Carla was sure she heard her mother's sigh of relief that matched her own. Once inside, an attractive man in a black suit greeted them. Carla recognized him from Anthony's funeral several years back. With only two funeral homes in town, most of those raised Catholic tended to gravitate here.

"I'm Frank Donato, and I'm so sorry for your loss. Right this way; we'll meet where it's a little cozier." He led them into a side office with a loveseat and several chairs around a table holding paperwork and several tissue boxes. Carla sat in the seat closest to him, while Trisha joined Betty Sue on the loveseat.

After introductions and expected small talk to break the ice, Mr. Donato opened a folder with Elena's name on it. "There's really very little you need to do this morning," he began. "Elena actually came in almost ten years ago and pre-planned most of the details."

"She did?" Carla asked incredulously. "I had no idea."

"She did stipulate that any changes you wanted to make were to take priority – but she didn't want this time to be a burden on you." He gave Betty Sue a sympathetic look. "She made the plans while you were in Tennessee, so any changes were left to Carla. I hope you understand."

Betty Sue blinked back tears, determined not to show how left out she felt. "Of course, I do...and bless her pretty little head for thinking of Carla like that." Trisha reached over and patted her hand reas-suringly.

Carla glanced over the notes in front of her, smiling at Elena's choice of music and flowers. *You picked your favorites, Nonna. I knew some of these, but I would have missed that last one.* Tears welled up once again at how much her grandmother had loved her, providing relief even after she was gone. "All of this looks perfect; they're her favorites."

Betty Sue, not wanting to be left out, tried to participate in the only way she knew how. "I'd like to cover the cost, if possible." Glancing at Carla, she added, "It's the least I can do."

Mr. Donato turned to Carla. "Your grandmother already paid for some of these charges, but there's a remaining balance, as well as those last minutes expenses that add up. Are you okay with your mother's offer?"

Carla nodded, meeting her mother's gaze. "Thanks. I wasn't sure if I'd have enough in the bank."

"I wish I could do more," Betty Sue replied. "I mean that, Carla...truly."

*But where were you all the years Nonna and I scraped by? Off farting around the world with your rich husband, never giving a thought to me. Never called for a single birthday or Christmas — just sent a guilt-ridden card with a few twenties in it. The big grand gesture now comes up a little short.*

While a part of her still wanted to scream the words and lash out with barbs, she lacked the energy to do so. Instead, she signed the needed forms and passed them to her mother, watching the credit card exchange hands and back. All the while, Trisha sat between them, giving nods of encouragement and serving as a silent mediator between them.

"There's only one item remaining," the funeral director said. "We have some information and could write a simple obituary, but often someone in the family prefers to complete that task."

"I'm not sure I'm the one to—"

Trisha interrupted with the solution. "Why not ask Jean to do that? She's known Elena all her life, and might have a little more objectivity."

"I think she'd like that," Betty Sue added, knowing enough not to offer herself.

After a warm goodbye to Trisha, with assurances for support whenever they needed it, Carla and Betty Sue returned home for a quick lunch before James Winston arrived. The scents of Elena's favorite soup filled the air, and Carla had to blink back tears once again. "Pasta e fagioli?"

"I've always used her recipe, and it seemed appropriate today," Jean said, ladling out four servings. "Hannah baked some fresh popovers as well. She'll eat with us and then head home. Come sit, and you can both fill me in on how things went."

Lunch was subdued, and Carla was content to eat while Jean and Betty Sue reminisced about growing up with Elena's recipes. Hannah sat with her, content to simply offer her presence as a gift to Carla.

Carla reached for a second popover, slathering butter on each piece as she ripped it open. "Thanks for these," she said to her friend. "It's like having Nonna right here again. And I didn't realize how hungry I was."

"I figured you probably hadn't eaten much last night. Promise me you won't let this stuff sit in the fridge and go bad, okay? I know you sometimes forget to eat when you're in a bad place."

"I promise," Carla replied, licking melted butter off her finger. "And I think Paul might come over later, so I can heat up some of the chili."

"There's cornbread, too," Hannah said. "You know my mom – she can't make chili without cornbread."

"Sounds like I won't have to cook for days. Considering what's ahead, I guess that's a good thing."

"Did you guys decide on a timeframe?"

Carla nodded. "Doing everything on Saturday. Visiting hours in the morning and then Mass and the cemetery. Nonna had the whole thing planned out – wanted a weekend so those fishing might have a better chance to come, and the ladies will do a luncheon back at St. Peter's Club."

"She must have done all that a long time ago," Hannah said. "Leave it to your Nonna to make things easier for you now. She was one special lady."

Betty Sue and Jean had paused in the conversation and heard Hannah's last comment.

"That she was," Jean offered. "And we're all better people for having known her." She stood up and gathered the empty bowls and plates. "Now why don't you two relax for a few minutes while Hannah and I clean up the kitchen? Jim will be here in about twenty minutes."

Carla slipped outside and sat on one of Nonna's old rocking chairs by a patch of weeds that had once been her garden. *I'll never forget all the veggies you grew here, Nonna. You had such a green thumb, and I never took to gardening, no matter how much you coaxed me.* She texted Paul, not sure he'd respond from work, but a reply came within a minute asking how she was doing. "Got through the funeral planning, and now waiting for the lawyer to go through whatever papers he has. Any chance you'd like to come for dinner later? Homemade lasagna and chili from the neighbors."

"Damn, those are good neighbors! And count me in. Should be there by six or so."

She sent back a quick reply, and got a heart emoji before Paul signed off. *It'll be good to see him after a long day. Please, Nonna, help me to not screw this up with him. I've never had a guy treat me so well, and I'm praying he sticks around – and petrified that he might. What if we finally have sex and then he takes off? I'm so scared, Nonna, and I don't like the feeling at all.*

"Carla?" Hannah had slipped outside. "Mr. Winston is pulling in, so I'm gonna head out and let my mom play mediator. Call me later if you wanna talk, okay?"

Carla welcomed the hug. "Thanks, bestie. For everything the past couple of days. And I'll call if I need you. Paul's actually coming over for some dinner, so I might be okay."

Hannah gave her an extra squeeze. "Promise me you won't jump into bed with him right away because you're lonely."

"Ah, he already told me basically the same thing. Wants to make sure I'm really ready and not just reacting to being alone."

"God, woman, you hold onto this guy. He's a keeper, for sure. See you Saturday, if not before."

As Hannah headed around toward the front of the house, Carla entered the kitchen to find the lawyer sitting down across from Jean and Betty Sue, leaving her the empty seat beside him.

"How's Arlene?" Betty Sue asked, settling in across from him. "I'll have to have her over to catch up after all this is behind us."

"I'm sure she'd like that," Jim said formally. "I have Elena's will and some other paperwork. I don't normally keep originals, but she asked me to hold them back when her dementia started. I thought you'd appreciate getting the legal issues dealt with quickly."

"I think that's very sensible, James," Betty Sue replied, turning her southern drawl up just a notch. "I'm sure my daughter will have a lot on her plate, and if I can help with cleaning out the house and selling it, I'd be happy to take that off her hands."

"Excuse me?" Carla snapped. "You're just gonna sell it? And shove me out on the street?"

"I assumed you'd finally want to leave – you've been talking about how much you hate this town for years."

"That's not the point! You don't seem to give a shit about whether I'd have a place to live or not!"

"Ladies, if I may," Jim Winston cut in before Jean could squelch the rising tension. "Betty Sue, while I appreciate your offer and concern, I'm afraid the decision's not yours to make, as the house belongs to Carla."

"Wait, what?" Carla's eyes were wide with shock. "What do mean, it belongs to me?"

The lawyer slipped a document out of his folder. "It's right in her will. She made sure to include it specifically as being left to you."

Betty Sue stared pensively at the document. "I guess I assumed it would come to me as her daughter."

"Why?" Carla rebuked. "You'd been gone for years when I started paying the bills. Why would she leave you a penny? You sure as hell don't need it with millions in the bank!"

"That's not fair! I can't help it if Kenneth became rich!"

Jean tried to keep things civil. "Ladies, Jim doesn't have time to sit and listen to you two squabble."

Both women sank back in their seats like students reprimanded by the principal. Jim Winston turned to the second page. "I'll continue with the will. Jean, she left you several paintings of Sicily—the ones in her bedroom—although she actually stipulates that you allow Theresa Rossi to choose one as well."

"Our ancestors all came from Sicily and settled here in the Fort. I'll be sure to let Terri take at least one."

"Betty Sue, you've inherited all her jewelry, with the exception of one silver locket that Carla always admired when she was a young girl."

"I remember," Carla said. "It has little vines carved on the front, and a picture of my grandfather inside."

"She wore it every Sunday to Mass," Betty Sue added. "I remember it, too. It was her favorite piece of jewelry. Was there...anything else?"

"Elena had some bonds, probably valued at several thousand right now, and some Italian coins, worth a little. But it all goes to Carla – including the house and all its contents."

"Everything? You mean she only left me her jewelry? Even though I grew up and lived here for so many years?"

"Oh, come off it, Mother! You walked away from everything in this house decades ago – including me! Why would Nonna leave you *anything?*"

"You have no—"

Jean glared at Betty Sue, who quickly closed her mouth without finishing. She sat with tight fists as James continued.

He skimmed through the other papers in front of him. "There are a few more things here. First, she left each of you a letter."

Carla watched him hand Betty Sue a pale blue envelope before giving her the same. She lovingly fingered her name written in her grandmother's cursive, dated many years prior. *Five years after Mom left; I would have been twelve.* She watched her mother studying her own letter before meeting her gaze. *What the hell did you have to say to both of us, Nonna?*

"I...think I'll save this to read later," Betty Sue murmured.

"One last item," Jim said, sliding another envelope toward Carla. "These are all US bonds which matured last year; Elena indicated they should be given to you after her death."

"But, you already said there were bonds."

"These were sent from your father, along with a letter he sent to Elena."

"My...dad?"

"*Brad?*" Betty Sue sounded even more surprised.

The lawyer nodded and continued with Carla. "He sent them regularly until your mother remarried, and then they stopped coming."

Carla's head was ready to explode. "I think I need some air." She slipped out the back door and curled up in Nonna's old chair. *First, the house ends up being mine, and now I find out my dad sent me money for years and there's a letter I never knew about? Why would Nonna keep them from me, knowing how alone I was feeling? What the fuck?*

She let the tears come. Angry tears. Bitter tears. Sad and salty tears. She sat silent and defiant as they dripped off her face, staring straight ahead into Nonna's old garden. It was Jean who finally came out to join her. "I left the file from the lawyer on the table for you to go through when you're ready. Your mother is coming back to my house, and I'll drive her home later, but if you need me, I'm right across the street." She gently placed her hand on Carla's shoulder. "I know it's a lot to take in, and I suspect you want some time alone right now."

Carla nodded, reaching up to squeeze Jean's hand. "Thanks for knowing me so well."

"Call if you need me; otherwise, I'll check in tomorrow, okay?"

Again, Carla nodded, knowing she didn't have to respond to the neighbor who been more of a mother than her own had ever been. It wasn't until Paul texted that she moved back inside, tucking the folder away on Elena's bedside table. *I'm not ready to read anything yet. Right now, I need a distraction, and Paul's the perfect person to take my mind off of the shitstorm going on inside my brain.*

# CHAPTER SEVEN

The next two days passed by in a blur with last minute tasks before the funeral. Carla leaned on Hannah, Jean, and Paul during visitation hours. Elena had chosen to be cremated, so her urn and photo adorned a blue velvet cloth that complemented the autumn colors of the floral arrangement. Carla had no energy to fight her mom on the flowers, but winced as they lined up for visitors, as Betty Sue turned on her Southern Belle and monopolized the viewing.

Most of her mother's friends, dubbed the "brunch club" by one of them, were sincere in their sympathy toward Carla, as they were well aware who the primary caregiver had been over the years. She was more surprised to see her boss Joey show up and envelop her in a bear hug.

"You doin' okay, Squirt?"

"I'm managing. Hope to get back to work on Monday."

"Hey…you don't come through that door until you're damn ready, got it? Place ain't the same without ya, but we'll get by till you're up for it."

Paul, who had been standing next to Carla, agreed. "The two old guys at the end get their own beer, and one of them was serving someone coffee yesterday."

"Rod and Bernie? Great, now my job's in jeopardy."

Joey grinned. "Hey, there's the sarcastic kid I love...you take of yourself, okay?"

"I will. And thanks for coming, boss."

"Can't stay – gotta get back to open up." He gave one more hug and then headed out the door.

"He's really concerned about you," Paul said. "Talked about you nonstop to a few at the bar last night. The regulars all agree that you're the one that keeps Joey going."

"I doubt that, but it was nice of him to come." Carla actually looked forward to going back to work – to boring routines and a crew she didn't have to worry about saying the wrong thing to. *Much as I complain about the place, it really is like a second home for me.*

She went back to watching her mother's theatrics as the last of the line passed through, and not soon after they loaded into cars and headed to the church, and then the cemetery. By the time they got back to St. Peter's Club near the church, Carla desperately wanted to be alone.

"You must be dying to get out of here." Hannah had caught up to her as they walked in the side door and down a few steps.

"Does it show that bad?"

"Not at all – you're doing great. But I know you, and I think you reached your people limit a couple of hours ago."

"My head is throbbing. I just wanna go home and curl up and try to finally sleep – except that hasn't worked too well the last couple of days."

"Read the letters yet?"

Carla shook her head. "Didn't have the energy – especially with today to get through, and my mom doing her Southern Belle drama. I swear, if I hear her say 'don't you worry your pretty little head about it' one more time, I'm gonna scream."

"Come sit with me and JJ and eat something; and sneak out whenever you need to."

"I'm not gonna leave early from Nonna's final goodbye – but I can't wait to get home."

She let Hannah lead her over to a table where JJ sat with a few others she'd grown up with. Kim McBride, Hannah's older sister, got up to give her a hug as Paul showed up with a small plate of food.

"I got you a few things to pick on," he said, putting a plate on the table in front of the empty chair beside his. As Carla sat down, Paul gestured toward the guy on his other side. "You know Bill, right? We've been hanging a lot lately; he's the first one who talked to me when I pulled into town."

"Hey," Carla said, amused at the idea of not knowing someone she'd grown up with on the piers of Harbor Cove and Pavilion Beach. "How's the champ these days?" Bill had won an annual event that summer called the Greasy Pole Contest, and earned some local accolades and lots of free drinks.

"Hey, I'm back to being just another fisherman again – and I'm glad to be out of the limelight."

Carla had noticed Kim wince a bit at the mention of "fisherman". She had lost her fiancé Anthony in a storm at sea several years back, and hated the industry ever since. Seated next to her was Anthony's younger brother Vinny, who had hated boats and the sea long before losing his brother.

"Thanks for coming, Vinny. Couldn't have been easy today."

"Hey, she was everyone's grandma at some point in our lives – I wanted to be here."

Carla noticed his nervous glances around the room, almost trying to be invisible. *His dad must have seen him here. Probably why he's sitting over on the far side of the room with his back to us. But I wonder if his mom will at least say hello?* Vinny had come out to his parents shortly before his brother's death, and without his sibling as a buffer, he found it unbearable living at home with parents who couldn't accept him for who he was.

"The Catholic Church has stupid rules," she blurted out. "But I understand what it's like to have parents choose something else over us."

Vinny nodded. "Yeah...I know you do."

Bill Peterson turned sympathetically to his old classmate. "Hey...I know we haven't seen much of each other since…Anthony…and I know it's gotta be hard watching me work with your dad in his place…but I miss you. I'd really like to hang out at some point if you're game."

Everyone at the table waited for Vinny's response, knowing the animosity that had grown between the two old friends.

"I'll think about it."

"Fair enough. You know how to find me."

Vinny turned his attention to Kim, Hannah, and JJ, and soon was engrossed in a conversation about tiny houses with the latter pair. Carla smiled, noting the way JJ winked at Hannah before answering Vinny's questions. *He might have been my heart throb in high school, but they clearly belong together. Besides, I might have finally found the one who will care for me that way.* Almost as though he read her thoughts, Paul turned and winked at her before continuing his conversation with Bill. For a brief moment, all the chaos and grief from the past few days faded away with Paul's presence beside her. *Please, Nonna. Let him stay, okay?*

After the luncheon, Betty Sue convinced the "brunch club" to come back to her place to catch up. "It's been far too long since we've all been together," she said. "And I *know* you'll all want to be there to support me with so much grief lately."

"She'll milk Elena's death all she can," Jean said to Kelly as they carried a couple of trays out the door with leftovers. She was glad to see Carla leaving with food and friends as well.

"Hey, at least at her place I know there'll be wine," Kelly replied.

Within minutes they all pulled into the lot by Betty Sue's townhouse, and as Kelly predicted, wine was poured not long after.

"They really should serve wine at funeral luncheons," Betty Sue complained. "It would make it easier to get through such a long day."

"Ain't gonna happen when you have the luncheon at St. Peter's Club. Maybe we should have gone to the Elks; could have had Bloody Marys." Kelly raised her glass. "To Elena − and all the love she gave to all of us."

Glasses clinked as all but one of the seven shared countless memories. Sharon Collins, the newest member of the brunch club, hadn't met Elena, but heard lots of stories in the short time she'd been around. Her son owned the townhouse next to Betty Sue, and she'd become friends with all of them over the summer.

"So how are things down in Caldwell?" Kelly asked. "We need to come back down and bring the rest of the gang; it was such a nice little town."

Sharon smiled. "I'd love that – and so would my dad. He still asks about you, and loved being the center of attention."

"Awww, he was a sweetie," Jean replied. "And boy, did he love to talk!"

"You should hear him now," Sharon said. "Last week he found out he's gonna be a great-grandfather. My son Tim and his wife Maggie are making me a grandma!"

A collective cheer was followed by more glass clinking.

"What a blessing!" Arlene Winston, the lawyer's wife, was the first to offer personal congratulations. "You'll be the first grandmother of our little group!"

"And it might be a while before anyone joins you," Jean added.

"Sure ain't gonna be me!" Peg Fernandez, the oldest – and never married – member teased.

"Or me," Kelly chimed in.

Sharon turned to Kelly. "That reminds me. What's been going on with Travis lately? Hadn't you two decided to date again not too long ago? You haven't said a thing."

Kelly placed her glass on the table and sighed. "Nothing to tell, unfortunately. We had a date all lined up to go hiking at Halibut Point, but then his boss decided to transfer him to the Chicago office for the next three to four months – I guess some project manager dropped dead on the job, and they felt Travis was the best person to fill in and find a replacement."

"Chicago's not the end of the world, you know – and flights wouldn't be that expensive for a few trips back and forth."

Kelly shook her head. "There's no way I'd fly out for a weekend – besides, him being in Chicago is like an extended business trip, and we all know I don't have a great feeling about him on business trips."

Terri agreed. "Yeah, if my husband cheated on me on a business trip, I would've walked out, too – unless I decided to feed him to the sharks instead."

Everyone chuckled except Kelly, who was deep in thought. "As for a reconciliation, we decided we'd put everything on hold until he was back – and then we'll start dating again to see if there's anything to save."

"I think Hannah and Carla are the only kids dating right now," Betty Sue said. "I guess it will come down to one of them to make any of us grandparents."

Arlene looked flustered. "Oh, I don't think Hannah is actually *dating* JJ; she's just his tutor."

"What, my daughter isn't good enough for your son?" Jean teased.

Arlene's cheeks flushed. "Oh, goodness, no – I think Hannah's delightful!" She fidgeted with her wedding ring as she continued. "It's just that James wants JJ to find a nice girl at church or the Elks. You know, one that shares the same beliefs."

Kelly laughed. "So. *James* doesn't approve of the little blonde pagan."

"It's not that—"

"Arlene, relax," Jean assured. "I don't think either of them are looking that far down the road right now – they're just enjoying each other's company."

Terri Rossi sat quietly, her own grief more pronounced during the past few days. "I bet Anthony and Kim would have had kids by now."

Silence swept away the laughter like a giant wave as the last funeral came rushing back.

Jean was the first to offer her friend solace. "They would have been great parents – and I would have loved grandparenting with you."

Terri exhaled, her sadness growing. "At least you still have a chance...I'll never get grandkids now with Vinny being..."

Her voice trailed off, so Peg chimed in. "For God's sake. Gay couples can still have kids, ya know."

Jean was more sympathetic. "Was it hard seeing him there today?"

Terri nodded. "Harder on Nate."

"Yeah, he looked super uncomfortable," Kelly said, "Although I wonder if you might have been more likely to talk to Vinny if Nate hadn't come."

"I'm not sure that'll ever happen," Terri murmured.

"Look, I know how much your faith means to you," Peg argued. "But are you really gonna let it come between you and your only living son?"

"It's not that simple," Arlene said, still fidgeting with her wedding ring. "I think Terri is also being a good wife, abiding by her husband's wishes."

"Can we just table this conversation?" Terri snapped. She tried to stand up, only to grimace and sit back down.

"You okay?" Peg was the first to ask.

"Damn sciatica, that's all. I'm fine. And today is about Elena, remember?"

Betty Sue raised her glass again, glad to have the attention back on her. "Terri's right, this day is all about Mother. And don't you worry your pretty little heads about me – I know I'll be just fine with my brunch club behind me."

Jean joined in the toast, but kept her eyes on Terri. *Yeah, we'll table this for now, my friend. But one of these days you and I are gonna have a long talk about you, the son you lost, and the one you're dying to reconcile with. Even if it does piss off your husband and the Pope.*

# CHAPTER EIGHT

Jean finished her coffee as the phone rang, wondering why Terri was calling so early. "What's up, lady? You don't usually call this time of day."

"Yeah, well if this damn physical therapy was doing its job, I wouldn't have to. Any chance you might have some time this morning?"

"What's going on? You sound like you're hurting."

"I can't put my friggin' shoes on," Terri spit out. "Sciatica is killing me, and I can't miss this appointment."

"If you need a ride, you've got it. What time?"

"Gotta leave in half an hour – might take me that long to walk out the door today."

"I'm on my way. Take a couple of pain pills and I'll put your shoes on when I arrive."

"Thanks. You know how much I hate asking for help."

"Glad you did. See you soon."

She scribbled a note for Hannah and Kim, grabbed a bottle of water, and pulled into Terri's driveway in ten minutes.

Knowing the door was likely unlocked, she rang the bell and opened it. "It's Jean. Your chariot awaits." She found Terri at the kitchen table, barefoot and holding a pair of socks. "Damn, I can see how much you're hurting. But where are the dogs? I was expecting more of a welcome."

"Nate took them on the boat; sometimes at home they try too hard to offer support and end up being in the way. Getting old sucks."

Jean knelt down with the socks in her hand. "Beats the alternative, though."

Terri grimaced as she lifted her right leg enough for Jean to slide her sock and shoe on. "Pain is so bad today. I think physical therapy is making it worse, not better."

Jean grabbed the corner of the table. "Give me a sec to stand up with this bad knee, and I'll help you out to the car. Doesn't Nate have a cane he uses for his back sometimes? You could borrow it."

"I ain't using no cane...just give me your arm." Swearing like a sailor as she stood, Terri took a deep breath. "Okay, the walking's probably the easiest part of this trip."

"Yeah, well considering the pain you're in, we'll take it slow."

Once out to the car, Jean opened the passenger side door and slid the seat back all the way. "It'll be easier to get in. Sit facing me, and I'll help with your legs." Terri grunted as she lowered herself to a seated position. "You ready? I'll be as gentle as I can be."

Terri closed her eyes and braced herself, almost calling out in pain as Jean rotated her legs into the car. "Shit, that hurt."

Jean gave her a sympathetic smile before closing the door and getting into the driver's side. She reached over and pushed a button. "You'll appreciate the heated seats. Is your doctor aware of how bad the pain is?"

"Believe me, he's heard plenty."

Jean chuckled as she headed back into town toward the medical building next to the hospital. "Did he tell you it would probably hurt more before you started noticing a difference?"

"Yeah, but how much longer? I can't do a damn thing around the house, and half the time Nate comes home after a long day to find nothing for dinner. I hate it!"

"Been doing the exercises at home?"

"Shit, you saw me. I can't put my damn *shoes* on! Stupid exercises aren't exactly a priority. Sorry I'm in a crappy mood; I'm just exhausted."

"Can't sleep?"

"I can't find a position that doesn't hurt. Been sleeping in the recliner half the time, and even that just takes the edge off. I'm ready to quit the whole therapy routine."

Jean glanced over as she drove. "Yeah, like that's gonna make the pain go away. Besides, you told me you had fight like crazy to get the cost down without insurance. So don't throw that money away on something that might still help."

"Whatever." Terri clammed up, and Jean let her sulk in silence. She had a bad knee and a back that occasionally gave her trouble, so she understood how pain could be all consuming.

"You may need some help at home," she offered as they pulled into the parking lot.

"Sure, I've got tons of money to pay for that, too."

"Hear me out. Hannah's between jobs right now with Elena gone, and she doesn't want to jump into something without scoping out what's around. I bet she'd love to come and help you out with the house – even cook a meal or two."

"We don't do charity, you know that."

"For God's sake, it's not charity. It's friends helping each other out. If you weren't so obstinate you might actually benefit." Jean pulled in right by the door and walked around to the passenger side, grabbing a wheelchair by the entrance first.

"I'm not using that thing," Terri said as Jean opened the door.

"Oh, the hell you're not," Jean replied, reaching in to grab Terri's legs. "Ready?" She gently rotated them up and out of the car as Terri clenched her jaw. "Look, your therapy is on the second floor, and you can hardly move. Swallow your damn pride and get your butt in the chair so you have some energy left inside. I swear you're more stubborn than I am."

Terri managed a chuckle as she let Jean help her maneuver from the car to the chair. "Compared to me, you're a lightweight. Now move your vehicle out of the fire lane. I can at least wheel myself in."

"Bet I catch up before you reach the elevator."

"Yeah, well don't run. All I need is for you to fall and screw up your knee. I swear, we're like the blind leading the blind."

"Hey, don't knock it. My one good knee is still better than both of your hips combined. Be right back."

Jean got Terri upstairs without incident, and pulled a book out of her purse. "I'll be out here reading – make sure you tell the doc how bad that pain is."

Jean texted Hannah while Terri was in therapy, and the latter agreed to help out at Terri's house as needed until she got another job. *Now I just have to sell the idea.*

It ended up being easier than she thought it would be, as Terri came out in more pain than when she went in.

"Damn doctors are trying to kill me," Terri complained on the way home. "Now they want me to go for an MRI to see if anything else is going on besides sciatica. Do they think I'm *made* of money?"

"You could apply for financial aid and most likely pay nothing. Most hospitals around here work with patients who have limited income."

"I told ya, Nate and I don't do charity. We'll either refuse whatever treatment there is, or spend the rest of our lives paying it off."

*Stubborn as a mule – both of you.* "So, what will you do in the mean time? You still have the issue of how to manage at home."

Terri didn't answer, and Jean decided not to push it. But once home, noting the pain Terri seemed to be in as they hobbled into the house, she decided to broach the subject again. After getting Terri settled into a recliner with a glass of water and some pills, Jean sat in the old wooden rocking chair beside her and took a deep breath.

"Look, I know how hard it is to ask for help; I've had to in the past and it was like getting teeth yanked out. But sometimes it's truly what you need, and maybe even what God is *sending* you. You're letting your own pride get in the way of a lesson you might need to learn about humility."

Terri stared down at the floor. "We can manage. We have been up to now."

"For God's sake, you're in *agony* right now! You've got people in your life who are offering to help — not because they pity you, but because they love you. You're basically spitting in their face by turning them down!"

Terri leaned her head back and closed her eyes, finally defeated. "Okay," she croaked out. "Maybe I do need some help."

"Hallelujah! There's hope for you yet," Jean replied. "Look, when you were in therapy, I texted Hannah about helping out — she can clean, do laundry, and cook some meals for you. And we can both help driving you to appointments. It'll give you time to rest and heal, and still have things done for you and Nate. Does that sound like a deal?"

"On one condition — she's not doing it for nothing. We can't pay a lot, but I refuse to let her come for free when she could be out getting a real job."

"I'm sure she'd be more than willing to accept those terms. I'll let you two figure it out, but give me a time for her to be here tomorrow and she'll arrive ready to work."

"Let's say ten. I've been going back to sleep after Nate leaves for the boat, so that'll be a good time to come and help do a little cooking and cleaning. I don't have physical therapy tomorrow."

"She can help with exercises here at home, too. Now, is there anything in your refrigerator right now for you two to have for dinner tonight?"

"I took some leftovers out of the freezer yesterday — we're good for tonight."

"Well then, I'm gonna head out and let you get some sleep — you look pretty wiped and those pain pills should be kicking in soon. Call if you need me for *anything*, got it?"

Terri nodded, and Jean patted her hand as she got up to leave. "Hang in there."

As she reached the door, Terri offered a one word reply. "Thanks."

When Jean got home, her oldest daughter Kim was pulling into the driveway right behind her. "Wow, you're home early. Not working at Hammond Castle tonight?"

"Nope; nothing going on until Saturday, so I have a normal work week with only one job."

"I don't know; judging from that pile you're carrying, I'd say you've brought work home with you."

"A teacher's job is never done; besides, I have parent-teacher conferences coming up next month, and I don't feel as organized as I'd like. Where have you been?"

Jean held the door open for as they entered the house. "Terri's. Her sciatica's so bad she can hardly move. Had to put her shoes on this morning before taking her to physical therapy."

"Poor thing. And I'm sure she's ignored it forever instead of getting it treated – she's such a stubborn woman."

"Who's stubborn?" Hannah asked from the kitchen, where she had a candle burning next to tarot cards laid out on the table.

"Terri – who else?" Kim walked over and inhaled deeply. "Hmm... smells really good whatever it is. Apple? Pumpkin?"

Hannah rotated the candle around. "Carrot cake. One of my favorite fall scents."

"So, who's the spread for? Those are some nice cards."

"JJ, actually – and you're right. He asked me to do one and bring the results; not sure his mom would approve if she walked in on me doing a reading in their family room."

"Oh, God," Kim said. "Definitely not! She'd probably ban you from being there. Such an evil influence on her son."

"Hey," Jean chided. "In fairness, that's not Arlene as much as it is Jim. He's the uptight one."

"I don't know, Mom," Hannah replied. "She doesn't seem to have any ideas of her own; everything is based on what 'James' wants. I kinda feel sorry for her."

"And yet you're over there an awful lot," Kim teased, wrapping her arms around her sister's neck from behind. "Must be that hot son of hers."

Hannah smiled, patting her sister's hands. "He is pretty damn hot; you won't get an argument from me."

Kim accepted a glass of iced tea that her mom had brought over to the table, and sat down next to Hannah. "So, are you two officially dating?"

"I guess. I mean, he kissed me last week, so I think we've taken it up a notch."

"I bet JJ's dad would blow a gasket if he knew his son was falling for a pagan."

Hannah took a picture of the spread with her phone and started putting her cards away. "That's why I plan on keeping that house a tarot-free zone. I don't want anything to screw up our time together."

"Speaking of tarot-free zones," Jean chimed in. "Terri accepted the offer for you to go over and help her out with cooking and cleaning. Said you could head over there around ten tomorrow."

"I'm glad," Hannah replied. "She looked like she was really hurting at the funeral. I'll try to make life a little easier for her." Turning to her sister again, she continued. "Granted, she'd rather have her 'sunshine' there I'm sure, but the other McBride will have to do."

"Give her my love, and tell her I'll stop by someday soon to visit."

"I'm sure she'd love that," Jean said. "She was talking about you and Anthony after the funeral, and wondering if you'd be having kids by now."

Kim almost glared at her mom. "Yeah, well obviously that didn't happen."

"What about you, big sis? Did you ever decide to go out with that dorky organ professor?"

"His name is Edward – and no, I haven't. I'm not quite ready yet."

Hannah chuckled. "For once, I'm glad to hear it. He's so damn stuck up, and thinks he's going to rescue you from the swamp of Gloucester."

"You could be a little nicer, sis. I know he's a bit of a snob, but he'd treat me nice."

"Who wants to settle for nice? You could do so much better than him –someone like—"

"Don't you dare say his name! I've said it a million times, I can't date another fisherman. Ever. Especially with Bill working on Nate's boat. It just...it won't ever happen, okay?"

Hannah picked up her deck and blew out her candle. "If you say so," she teased, walking toward the hallway. Before leaving the room, she leaned back and grinned. "But in the style of that dorky Edward Pennington, I do believe the lady doth protest too much."

# CHAPTER NINE

Carla returned to work the following week, wanting a sense of normalcy in her life again. Joey welcomed her back with a warm hug, and the regular customers offered condolences and told her it was great having her back to keep Joey in line.

"Place wasn't the same without ya, Squirt," Joey said later that night. "You're the glue that keeps it all running."

"Yeah, right; I'm a friggin' waitress," Carla said, mopping the last section of the floor.

"Hey, don't put yourself down like that, ya hear? You could seriously run this place – if you had a decent cook."

"We haven't had one of those the whole time I've worked here." She ducked when Joey threw a wet bar rag her way. "You know I'm kidding, boss." She came behind the bar and hung up her apron. "Thanks for covering for me – it's good to be back."

"Kinda lonely at home?"

"Yeah, it'll be hard going home to an empty house. She drove me crazy with her memory crap, but I still loved her smile every night when I walked in the door."

"Sit," Joey said, gesturing toward a bar stool. "Have a beer with me before you head out." He grabbed two frosted mugs and filled them from the tap. "Done any thinking about what you're going to do now? You always told me as soon as your nonna was gone, you were out of here."

"I know – but I didn't expect she was going leave the house to me."

"You can't be too surprised; you've been living there with her most of your life."

"I figured my mother would get it first. Especially after me talking about leaving for so long. But now it's actually *mine*."

"A homeowner, huh? Well, congrats!" Joey clinked his mug against Carla's. "Makes it a little harder to take off, then. If Elena was still alive, I'd have to thank her for that."

"Know what else? Turns out my *dad* sent me savings bonds for five years after he left. And a letter. I thought he walked away without looking back."

"Sounds like some deep stuff you're dealing with. If you ever need to talk, you know I'm here, right?"

Carla grinned. "Yeah, I know. You're the bomb, Joey."

Before her boss could answer, Paul walked in. "Hoped I might catch you before you left. How's my girl?"

*Your girl? Did you just call me your girl? I've never been anyone's girl before. A hook up, maybe, but a girl? Damn, I like the sound of that.*

Paul walked up behind Carla and wrapped his arms around her, leaning down to kiss her cheek. "Wanted to see how your first day back was."

Joey answered first. "Place is finally running like it should again – and I can start hiding out in the kitchen where I belong."

Both Carla and Paul laughed. "He's the best boss in the world," Carla said. "And it was good for me to come back to work."

"Speaking of which, your shift ended thirty minutes ago, and the place is closed. Why don't you two skedaddle and let me get outta here?"

"Thanks for the beer, Joey. See ya tomorrow."

"Night, Squirt. And Paul, I'm glad you came to town."

"Me, too," he replied, as he and Carla headed out the door. Once outside, he pulled her close. "Was thinking about you all day; I'm glad it was a good one. I suspected it would be."

"Being right here kinda helps, too." She leaned her head against his chest and breathed in the smell of the docks she'd grown up on. "Nothing like the smell of engine grease and dead fish at the end of the day."

Paul laughed. "And here I thought that's what you've been wanting to get away from all your life?"

Carla shrugged. "Sometimes the right person can give a different perspective on life."

"So...did you read the letters yet?"

"Couldn't do it last night. I almost opened Nonna's, but holding it and seeing her handwriting was too hard. And my dad's? I'm way too scared to open that one."

"If it would help to have someone there, I'd be happy to come and hold your hand."

"I might take you up on that. But tonight? I don't think I have the energy. Much as I'd love to fall asleep in your arms, I don't think it's the right time yet."

Paul exhaled deeply and hugged her tightly. "You have no idea how much I want that, but I agree with you on the timing." His lips brushed hers gently, and then with passion. "Now get out of here. Before I change my mind and take you home to bed."

Once home, Carla opened the refrigerator and scanned the remaining leftovers from the funeral luncheon. *Probably have to throw out some of this if it doesn't get eaten in the next day or so.* She pulled open some baked ziti and took a sniff, and guessing it was still okay, spooned some into a bowl and warmed it in the microwave. She curled up in Nonna's chair in the living room and clicked on the television for some noise, eating slowly as she scanned the room.

*So, all this is mine now. Some of it I love, Nonna, but there's some stuff that's really not me at all. How long do I have to wait before tackling some remodels without disrespecting you?* She clicked through the stations, not really caring what was on, and found some reruns of the Golden Girls. *One of your favorites.*

Though tired, she decided it was time to read the letter from her father. It was addressed to her grandmother, but inside there was a note to Nonna attached to another letter still sealed in an envelope with her name on it. "I'll leave it to you to decide on the right time, but this is for Carla to read someday. Brad."

*You never gave this to me, Nonna...why? God, I wish I knew what you were thinking.*

With trembling hands, she opened the envelope and pulled out a two page hand written letter. It was dated back when Carla was seven, a couple of months after Betty Sue had left her with Elena to run off with Kenneth. Taking a deep breath to calm the butterflies in her stomach, she read words written by the father she'd never known.

*Dear Carla,*

*I have no idea when exactly you'll read these words — if ever — but I trust your grandmother to make that decision. She sent me a note to tell me about your mom's upcoming wedding, and said you'll be living with her at least for a while. She also told me that your new stepfather is quite wealthy, so I'll be trusting your mom to make sure all your needs are met when she's traveling, and once she gets home and you have a new dad to take care of you.*

*I'm sure you have questions about me; I'm not sure if your mom ever told you much, but how I loved you, Little One. That first day at the hospital was one of the happiest of my life. Right from the start, you were belting your opinions out — waving those tiny little fingers about...I could have held you forever. But over the first couple of years, it became clear that your mom and I weren't a good fit, and I wasn't in a position to give the two of you the life she wanted us to have.*

*I'm a simple man, Carla. I make a living as a carpenter and boat builder, and will never aspire to be any bigwig or anything; I only need enough to live on. Your mom? She wanted so much more for both of you, and as time went on, all we did was argue, and I couldn't make her happy anymore. I stayed because of you — but after a couple of years, all the fighting was changing me, and I wasn't being a good husband or a father.*

*The day I left, your Nonna gave me a photo of you, and I'll treasure it always. I've sent bonds whenever I could to hopefully help you someday — whether it be for college or something special you want. I'm sure your new daddy will give you everything I couldn't — you deserve that. I hope he makes your mom happy; that's all I ever wanted for her. She's a little selfish sometimes, but she loves with her whole heart when she feels safe and secure.*

*If you do read this someday, and want to know more about me, your Nonna should have my address. I'm sorry I wasn't there for you in person, but I'll sure be thinking of you in the years ahead. Be happy, Little One.*

*Your dad*

Carla could hardly read the final words through her tears. *He wanted me. So why did he still walk out on us? And why didn't Nonna let me have this earlier? It might have made such a difference to know he at least loved me.* Memories of countless one night stands crashed in her mind; no amount of sex ever made her feel loved or wanted, and now a few hundred words made her feel like she mattered.

Anger joined the party of emotions inside her head. *I don't know if I'm angrier at Mom or Nonna. If Mom hadn't been so greedy about having money, maybe he would have stuck around. And if Nonna had given this to me earlier, maybe I wouldn't have been the town tramp. And Dad...would you wanna see me all these years later?*

She grabbed the outer envelope and found a post office box listed as his address in Peggy's Cove, Nova Scotia. Somewhere up in Canada, her father might actually still love her. *Do I dare find out? My God, what if he doesn't want me anymore? Is it better to just let it go?*

She was drained, and carried the letter into Elena's bedroom, propping it up against the lamp on the nightstand. She crawled under her grandmother's quilt and turned out the light, staring at the envelope in the dark until her eyes finally closed.

# CHAPTER TEN

Betty Sue had avoided Elena's letter for over a week, but with another empty day on her calendar, she curled up on her balcony, sipping her coffee in preparation.

"So, why did you save this instead of mailing it to Tennessee, Mother? You wrote this right after Kenneth built our house down there."

She opened the envelope and noticed a few photos, but the familiar handwriting enticed her to pull out the letter. With sweaty palms, she could almost hear her mother's voice.

*Dearest Betty Sue,*

*Your Christmas card arrived with a photo of the finished house, and I wonder if it will mean a new home to offer your daughter. You've traveled the world, lived every dream with that rich husband of yours — and your little girl has been growing up. Here are a few photos showing what a young lady she is:*

Betty Sue pulled them out of the envelope. "Bless your pretty little head...I've never seen these." She noticed ages scrawled on the back of each. One showed Carla at age nine, kneeling in Elena's garden holding a huge zucchini. Another at age eleven down at Pavilion Beach, arm in arm with Hannah, posing with sunglasses and goofy expressions on their faces as the waves crashed behind them. The last at age twelve, stirring a pot of pasta e fagioli with a pile of measuring cups, veggie scraps, and utensils all over the countertop. *Look at that mess...but what a proud smile. I remember when I was first taught that recipe.* Feeling nostalgic, she continued reading.

*I worry about her, Betty Sue. She's almost a teen, and she needs her mother – especially after you pushed her father away all those years ago. I wonder if he would have been a better parent for her. At least she might have felt wanted.*

"How dare you! To say that Brad would have been a better parent! He had trouble scraping pennies together, never mind providing for his wife and daughter!" She stared across the harbor to where her mother had lived. "It's a good thing you didn't give this to me earlier – I would have thrown it back in your face!" She took a gulp of coffee and held the letter back up. "Let's see what other nonsense you had to say..."

*I don't expect this note will change anything, and it's the last time I'll plead with you to make things right with her. She's a smart, sassy, and independent young lady, and I only pray I can give her what she needs. Jean has stepped in as a substitute mom, and I suspect Carla will rely on her more and more.*

Betty Sue winced at the mention of Jean as her replacement—she knew Carla had a strong bond with her. For the first time, a nagging sensation churned inside, but she couldn't quite identify the feeling.

*Someday, you'll regret missing out on her life. You never liked being alone, but if you don't make amends, you might end up an old woman, with nothing but bitter regrets about a child you missed out on knowing and loving.*

The churning continued, almost blossoming as a new emotion for Betty Sue – and her mouth became dry as her heartbeat began pounding.

*I doubt I'll send this letter – somehow, I don't think my words will mean a thing to you. I'm not sure they ever have.*

"You didn't even sign it, Mother!" Betty Sue folded up the letter and pulled her hands in under the blanket, still clinging to the paper as the final layers inside burst open to reveal the truth. Guilt. As she finally put a name to the sensation, her cheeks flushed and her hands shook.

She pulled the blanket around her as the tears spilled outward. "My

God... you're right. I never came to visit, or tried to help. I had all that money and never sent more than a pithy offering...I could have... supported you both...and it wouldn't have made a dent in my money."

*When did I get so selfish? All I cared about was making Kenneth happy, so he'd never leave me broke, like we were growing up.* Her blanket couldn't keep out the cold from creeping inside. She sobbed as her mother's words made an impact. *I'm beginning to understand how much richer you two were, working your butts off to make ends meet, but content with what you had. Me? I had everything, but it never satisfied me.* She shivered at her epiphany. "It still hasn't. You were always too busy working to take care of me, but I never learned how to be independent like Carla."

*That's why I was always chasing after men who promised to take care of me--even my Sean, who turned out to be a disaster. What am I going to do now?*

Still crying, she carried her coffee inside and placed it on the counter before curling up in bed under her expensive quilt. Self-discovery was draining, and Betty Sue closed her eyes, trying to avoid any more difficult truths she wasn't ready to face.

––––––––

She woke up hours later, somewhat rested but extremely hungry. *God, I need that coffee I didn't drink this morning. And some breakfast – or brunch, I guess.* The idea of brunch always brought her friends to mind, and she picked up her phone to see who might be available. Kelly and Peg were working, Terri had physical therapy, and Jean didn't pick up. That left Arlene. *She's either at home or some church function. Besides, what if she gets all preachy about the whole Sean fiasco? Still...she'd be the most likely to be free.* After a short deliberation, she decided brunch with Arlene would be better than being alone. She dialed the number, and Arlene picked up on the second ring.

"Winston residence."

"Arlene? It's Betty Sue. I was wondering if you might by any chance be free for lunch today? My treat, of course." *A free meal is always enticing – especially for Arlene.*

Instead, she was disappointed. "I'm sorry, Betty Sue – really I am.

But it's laundry day, and I can't afford to take a few hours away and still finish up before James gets home."

Not giving up, Betty Sue offered another solution. "I totally understand. But what if I were to bring lunch to you? I'm sure you could manage a short break in between switching loads over, couldn't you?"

Arlene didn't answer right away. "I don't know, sometimes lunch drags on—"

"Oh, don't you worry your pretty little head about that," Betty Sue lied, determined to win her over. "I have an appointment later on, so I could only stay for an hour or so. Honest."

Another pause. "I suppose an hour wouldn't be too—"

"Wonderful! I'll stop and pick up lunch on the way. Be there soon. Bye, Arlene!"

She hung up before Arlene could mount another protest. *Maybe she's not as fun as Kelly, but I think Arlene will appreciate having a special treat for lunch.* She took a quick shower, feeling a bit revitalized, and decided on lobster bisque and fresh croissants for lunch.

Within the hour, she pulled into the Winston's driveway, watching the squirrels scurry across the autumn blanket covering the cemetery across the street. *So pretty this time of year...but so blustery up here on the hill.* Normally, she'd take a moment to admire the view of Gloucester Harbor from Arlene's home, but today's chill urged her to grab the bag beside her and dash to the door.

"Come in out of the cold!" Arlene helped her with her coat and hung it up immediately in the front hall closet before taking the bag her friend offered. She felt the warmth from the bottom of the bag as she sniffed the contents inside. "Chowder?"

"Bisque – and croissants."

She knew Arlene would smile. "Perfect for a chilly day. Come to the kitchen and I'll get some bowls for us." Arlene led her through the dining room where an ironing board was set up in the corner and several piles of underwear and socks were stacked on the table. "James would probably disapprove of using the dining room, but I love the sun pouring in this time of year."

In the kitchen, Arlene got bowls, plates, and utensils while Betty Sue made herself comfortable at the table. "I'm so glad you were available on such short notice. I didn't want to be alone today."

Arlene joined her. "I've been praying for you, losing Elena right after Sean's arrest. I'm sure it hurts a lot having someone you love turn out to be nothing but a crook. How are you doing?"

Betty Sue smiled. *Maybe she's not as fun as Kelly, but her heart is always so concerned for each of us.* She reached over and patted Arlene's hand. "Don't you worry your pretty little head about that fiasco. I'm grateful he was discovered before cleaning me out for good." She accepted the steaming bowl from Arlene and picked up her spoon.

"Um, we always say grace in this house."

"Of course you do. And I appreciate that about you."

She bowed her head as Arlene folded her hands. "Dear Lord, I want to thank you for this wonderful meal, and the wonderful friend who brought it here. Please watch over her in the days to come, and guide her in her grief and healing. Amen."

"That was lovely. Thank you."

Arlene blew on her bisque, taking a small taste. "Hmmm. This is heavenly for such a chilly day. So how are you doing after losing Elena? I'm sure that's a much heavier burden than Sean."

Betty Sue winced and took a quick bite of croissant to avoid answering right away. *And here I thought this might be a nice distraction today, and instead she's pushing me right back into the guilt I felt all morning.* "It's been...harder than I expected."

"I imagine there were a lot of words left unsaid between the two of you after so many years apart."

"You have no idea," Betty Sue admitted. "Actually, she *did* get a chance to tell me what she thought. She'd written a letter to me years ago; your James had it in her files for me after she passed."

"But that's a gift straight from heaven!"

"Well, it sure didn't feel like a gift," Betty Sue replied, blinking back tears. "More like a trial. She made me realize I've been the world's worst mother. And I don't know how to fix it."

"You have to give it time. Carla will come around. I think you both want the same thing; but there's a lot of hurt to work through."

Betty Sue focused on the warm liquid running down her throat for several minutes before answering. "This morning, I just felt so alone, you know?"

Arlene paused, stirring the bit of bisque left in her bowl rather than eating it. "I think I can understand a little a bit about how that feels."

"Whatever do you mean? You have James, and JJ."

Arlene leaned back with her hands in her lap. Betty Sue noticed her fidgeting with her wedding band – a nervous habit that often accompanied talk about marriage. "Are things okay between you and James?"

"Of course they are!" More fidgeting. "James is a good provider, and he bought this lovely home, and worked hard at keeping JJ from going to jail. He's a real man of God."

Betty Sue wasn't convinced. "He doesn't strike me as being very amorous, though."

"Well, I'm not a hopeless romantic like you are. I'm a practical woman, and I try to be grateful for everything I have."

"Sounds like you might feel more alone here than I do in my empty townhouse. I'm not sure which is worse."

Arlene stood up and started clearing her bowl. "I, um, really have to get back to the ironing. I need to make sure it's all put away so I have time to straighten up before making dinner. I did so appreciate the lunch, though. Truly."

*So, I'm being dismissed. I guess I hit a nerve as well.* "You keep the leftovers for another lunch. And call me – any time you need to talk, or have a friendly face bring you lunch. My days are pretty open right now."

Arlene gave her a warm hug at the door. "I'll keep praying for you, my friend – especially for reconciliation. I know how hard it is to make things right with our children."

Betty Sue nodded. "I guess you do."

"I once thought JJ was gone forever, and yet here he is, back at home. There's still a lot to fix, but at least he's here. Maybe God has a miracle for you and Carla as well."

Betty Sue stepped out into the chill as the winds picked up. *Or maybe there's only another storm on the horizon between us. Keep praying, Arlene. I might need all the help I can get to have Carla forgive me.*

# CHAPTER ELEVEN

Carla had put off reading Elena's letter for too long, and on Saturday morning, she curled up under her grandmother's quilt and held the envelope in her hand. *I'm almost afraid to open this, Nonna. Like as long as your words are still sealed up inside, I have a piece of you that's almost alive and breathing. Once I've read them, it'll be the last time I ever hear your voice.*

"And if that doesn't show you how screwed up I am, I don't know what will," she said out loud to the letter. "I'm sitting here having a conversation with a friggin' envelope." She reached for her coffee mug and took a long swig. Looking at Elena's photo by the bedside, she exhaled and sat straighter. "Okay, Nonna, I'm as ready as I'll ever be."

She opened the letter and immediately caught her breath as her grandmother's lavender scent wafted from the paper inside. Holding it close to her nose, she inhaled deep and slowly, already reaching for the tissue box she'd just replaced a few days ago. *Come on. You've got this. Just rip off the band aid and read the damn thing.* Sinking back into the pillows behind her, she noted the date – like Brad's note, it was written when she was twelve.

*My dearest Carla,*

*If you're reading this, I'm most likely gone – unless I can muster up the courage I'm lacking right now. I just finished writing a letter to your mother; another one I may never send. Your Nonna's not as strong as you think I am.*

*This week I received two items in the mail that revolve around you, and my mind is swirling about what to do. No matter what I decide, I'm afraid you'll somehow get hurt, and that's the one thing I've tried to keep from you all these years. You've already gone through far more than any child should have to endure. I can sense how much you need your momma right now, and while I'll forever give you everything I can, I know I can't fill that space.*

*The first letter was from your mother, telling me about the new house, but never mentioning when you might move down there. She loves you — that I know. But she's always needed a man to make her feel safe and secure, and sadly she's always equated love with money. Your grandfather worked hard to put food on our table until he died, but your mom never felt like we had enough. She never realized she had everything she needed right here in the Fort — family, friends, love, and all the basics.*

Carla gazed at the wedding photo of her grandparents on the wall. "We really did have all that right here, didn't we?" She fingered the different patches on the quilt, remembering parties on Pavilion Beach with Jean, Hannah, Kim, and all the "Brunch club" friends and children who had become more like family. She was an only child raised by her grandmother, but she was never without siblings or adults who cared about her. "I wish I'd realized it back then...it was just so hard without either Mom or Dad around."

*I worry about you in the years ahead; I see you wanting more as well, and I'm so afraid you'll be like her and turn to any man who promises what you don't have now. You have an inner strength your mom doesn't have, and I pray it will guide you and give you the independence she never learned.*

Carla's eyes teared up as other memories resurfaced — this time not so pleasant. *Oh, Nonna, I did exactly that — too many times to count. All I wanted was for someone to tell me I was beautiful — but they all lied. I might have some inner strength now, but only because I built up a wall to keep everyone out, so I wouldn't get hurt anymore.* Carla stopped to wipe her tears on the quilt, pulling the warmth around her as she continued reading.

*So why am I writing all this today? I told you I got two items in the mail, and the other letter was more of a surprise. Your father, Bradley Douglas, sent me a letter, along with a sealed envelope with your name on it. He told me he'd trust me to give it to you when the time was right, and my dear Carla, I just don't know if the time will ever be right.*

Carla's stomach knotted in anger. "Yeah, I'd say you screwed up on that one, Nonna. You should have let me read me it back then – when I really needed it." Despite the anger, she eagerly read on, wanting to learn every detail she could about the author of her last letter.

*Your father is a good man, and I so hoped he could give your mother the peace she sought. However, I sensed early on he would never be "enough" for her. She was always looking beyond our little village and the simple life with basic pleasures. When you were born, I thought she'd come around and see what a wonderful life she had. A man who was not only loyal and hard-working, but one who fell in love with his little girl from the moment he first held you.*

*What a daddy he was to you! He'd come home after working all day and walk you around the house, singing Bob Seger and Doobie Brother songs at the top of his lungs – and for him, being with you and your mom was all he ever wanted. I wish she felt the same.*

Carla's tears were flowing through loud sniffles. "That's why I love Seger and the Doobies so much? Because of him?" She tried to remember the missing memories to explain her love of his music.

*One night, everything changed. Their argument started long before dinner, and ended late, out in the backyard. She spent an hour telling him he'd never amount to anything, and she wished he'd go away so she could find someone else. I don't think she expected he'd actually go.*

"What the hell?" Carla's tears dissipated in her anger. "*Mom* told him to leave? When all this time I thought he was a deadbeat who abandoned us?"

*No matter what happens in the years ahead, I will always be here for you. And whenever you finally read this letter, I hope it's a positive message, and might allow you to meet him again.*

*Please be the strong one and reach out to your mother. She doesn't have the backbone you do, but she loves you. I know she does. And Carla – my lovely Carla – never forget that you are ALWAYS enough. –Nonna*

Carla resisted the urge to crumple up the letter, throwing it instead onto the other side of the bed. Anger exploded inside of her, but with Elena gone, there was only one person to direct it toward. She picked up her phone and started dialing, but stopped halfway. Her heart was racing. "No...this time you get no prior warning, Mommy Dearest. I've got a few things to say to you, and it's about damn time you heard it all." She grabbed her jeans and changed, remembering to grab the letter and her phone before heading off to surprise her mother at the townhouse.

She pressed the doorbell, waiting only about two seconds before pushing it again. And again. By the time Betty Sue opened the door, Carla was primed.

"Carla, this is a big sur—"

Carla stormed past her without returning a greeting, but spun around as soon as Betty Sue closed the door. "Do you take pleasure in all the ways you ruined my life? Sit up at night and wonder, 'Gee, how can I screw up my kid a little more?' Ever stop to think about my needs? Just once?"

Betty Sue recognized the letter as the stationary matched the one she'd gotten. "I guess Nonna had a mouthful to say to you as well. Have a seat, and you can ask your questions."

"I don't wanna sit!" Carla spat out, pacing around the couch as Betty Sue sat down. "Yeah, I've got a great question for ya, *Mother!*" She almost hit her in the face with the letter she held. "Were you ever gonna tell me *you* were the one who made him leave – and he didn't abandon me like you said?"

Betty Sue shrank back on the couch, her face paling to the color of the cushions behind

her. "That's...not quite what hap—"

"Let me refresh your memory," Carla hissed as she started to read. "She spent an hour telling him he'd never be good enough for either of you, and she wished he'd just go away so she could find someone who was." Carla glared over the top of the paper shaking in her hand. "Should I read the whole damn thing to you? Might be quite enlightening!"

Betty Sue pulled a cushion in front of her, resting her head on top as the tears came.

"You think turning on the tears is gonna bother me? It might work with your friends, and all the men you need so much, but it's never worked on me, and it sure as hell isn't gonna start now!" Carla wheeled around and stormed out onto the deck, breathing in the salt air to quiet her rage and ignore the sobs coming from inside.

*No, you're not gonna get to me. Nonna's wrong – I don't think you ever loved me, and I have no desire to be the strong one here.* She stepped back inside, keeping her distance. "Nonna told me about my dad, and how much he loved me, and wanted a family. But you were never content with having love and simple things, were you?"

"The problem was bigger than that." Betty Sue stood and took a step toward her daughter. "We were barely scraping by; I knew he'd make more money with a job in the city. Any wife would encourage her husband to better himself!"

"Give me a break!" Carla said. "He was happy here! And you say barely scraping by, but you had *enough*! You're the one that wanted to move – so you could have more!"

"Don't you go accusing me of being the only one who wanted out of this town!" Betty Sue rebuked, thrusting her finger toward her daughter as her own voice rose. "All I've heard out of your mouth since I got back was how you couldn't *wait* to get out of here! You might be more like me than you think!"

Carla pushed her mother backwards, her chest heaving. "I will *never* be like you, always expecting others to fix things for you! I must be more like the *dad* you chased out of town!"

Betty Sue caught her balance before falling back onto the couch. She grabbed a pillow and threw it hard at her daughter. "Well, fine then! Why don't you just *leave* yourself and try to find him? Nothing's holding you back now, is there? Nonna's gone, so you can have a perfect little Hallmark reunion!"

She almost expected Carla to come after her with the pillow she caught, but anger turned to sarcasm as Carla stepped toward her with a twisted smile instead. "Maybe I'll *do* that, Mother. I could take a little trip up to Nova Scotia."

"What do you mean?"

Carla enjoyed the pain in her mother's eyes. "Oh, aren't you curious now? Remember that letter Mr. Winston gave me? Turns out my daddy wrote me the sweetest letter about how much he wanted me. And told me where to reach him. So maybe I *should* have a little Hallmark reunion – with the one parent who cared about me."

Betty Sue shivered at her cold demeanor. "Honey...I care, too! I know I've screwed up, but you don't understand everything. I can explain--"

She reached out for Carla, but instead dodged the pillow being thrown back at her. "Save the drama! I don't have to deal with you anymore, got it? In fact, I don't think I've ever hated you more than I do right now!"

Betty Sue panicked as Carla passed by. "Don't leave me, Carla! Please, we can work it out! I *do* love you, honest!"

Carla ignored the pleas and slammed the door so hard on her way out that she startled the woman getting out of the car next to hers.

"Carla?" The slender gray haired woman asked. "Everything okay?"

"Never better!"

Sharon Collins watched her back out, pulling out with squealing tires as she tore out of the parking lot. She'd just arrived for a visit to her son's condo next door to Betty Sue, and had plans later in the day to see Kelly for dinner. Instead of taking her overnight bag out of the car, she dialed Kelly's number and left a message. "Hey, I just arrived, and Carla came storming out of her mom's condo in a rage. I'm gonna stop over and see if Betty Sue is okay. Call you in a bit."

She knocked on her neighbor's door, and when no one answered, she tried the knob and found it unlocked. "Betty Sue? It's Sharon. Are you okay?"

Uncontrolled sobbing provided the answer, and she found her friend curled up on the couch clutching a now wet pillow. "She...hates me...and she should!"

Sharon sat down and extended her arm, inviting her friend over for a caring hug. "Come on...let it all out, lady...and then you can tell me about it." She stroked Betty Sue's back as bits and pieces came out between gasps and wails. Letters. Brad. Lies. Canada. She didn't even try to make sense of any of it, knowing that sometimes you simply had to release it all, and Betty Sue clearly had lots stored up to let go of.

# CHAPTER TWELVE

Carla didn't want to drive back to an empty house, so she went to the one other place that felt like home. Joey was wiping down an almost empty bar. "Hey, Squirt, what are you doing here on your day off?" As the tears started, his demeanor softened and he held out his arms. "Hey, hey, hey...come here, kid. What the hell has you so upset?" He held her, knowing she wouldn't answer until she was good and ready. "Shh...it'll be okay. I know it's not love troubles, cause he's right here playing pool."

"Paul's here?" Carla sniffled and wiped her eyes. "Right now?"

"Yep...playing pool with Bill. I'm glad Bill's found another friend – took him a long time after Anthony died to laugh again." Joey lifted Carla's chin to meet her gaze. "So, what's got you going today? Missing Nonna?"

"My mom." Carla replied. "Everything that's built up over the years just exploded tonight."

"Must have been a hum-dinger of a fight. Feel better for getting it all out?"

Carla grabbed some iced water and climbed on a bar stool. "I still feel crappy. Go figure."

Joey smiled and hung up the bar towel. "Did you ever consider maybe deep down inside you don't hate her after all?"

"Don't even go there, boss."

"If you say so, Squirt. At least not tonight."

Bill and Paul rounded the corner from the back area before Carla could answer.

"Hey!" Paul's pace picked up as a smile lit up his face. "What the hell are you doing here today?" He gave her a kiss. "Not that I'm complaining, mind you."

"Huge fight with my mom. Didn't wanna be sitting around at home by myself, and I didn't want the counseling I'd find across the street."

Bill chuckled. "You must be talking about Jean. I think she's counseled all of us over the years. Wish her daughter could be more like her."

"I suspect you're referring to Kim and not Hannah?"

"Ahh, Kim," Paul said. "I only met her once at the funeral, but I've sure heard plenty." He grinned at Bill and gestured toward the bar stools. "Mind if we sit for a few before heading out?"

Bill answered by pulling out a stool and asking Joey for a few beers. "Hey, I got all day; the boat's not going anywhere."

Carla looked perplexed. "What boat?"

"Can we tell her?" Paul asked. "I know she won't say anything."

"Ooooh, a *secret* boat!" Carla answered with a grin. "Please, count me in – I need cheering up."

"Okay," Bill replied, "But please don't say anything to anyone—not even Hannah. I don't wanna mess anything up."

Carla accepted one of the beers that Joey plopped on the bar and raised her glass. "I have no idea what the hell you're talking about, but my lips are sealed. To secret boats!"

Joey headed back to the kitchen, and Paul pulled his own stool over right next to Carla to form a close knit triangle between the three of them. His voice was hushed, but excited. "So, here's the deal. Bill's been looking into other opportunities to make money rather than fishing, and we've been talking about buying a lobster boat together and turning it into some kind of recreational boat – tours, parties, or something else. A boat just went up for sale, and we're gonna go and at least look at it."

Carla sipped her beer pensively. "So," she asked Bill. "This wouldn't have anything to do with a certain lady who says she'll never date a fisherman again, does it?" A grin crept onto her face, and she met Bill's gaze over the top of her glass. "If it does, your secret's safe with me – and I hope you get the boat renovated as fast as you can."

Bills face flushed a bit. "That obvious, huh?"

"To anyone that knows you, yeah. But what about Nate? You can't quit on him. He needs you."

"Look, Nate's really slowing down," Bill replied. "We're only going out a few days a week now, and they're shorter days. I think he needs to retire soon, and maybe if I'm not there, it'll help him decide."

"Hel-*lo!* Do you really think Nate will walk away from fishing? It's in his blood."

"That's what worries me," Bill said, his tone more somber. "He's real shaky sometimes, and God forbid if anything happens when we're miles from land."

"Shit, I never thought about that," Carla said. "Must be scary as hell for you."

Bill finished his beer. "I don't want to ever face a wreck again."

"Can you imagine Terri?" Carla said. "If anything happened to Nate out there?"

"That's why I really want this boat thing to work – for all of us. And I won't abandon Nate."

"Yeah, I know you won't," Carla admitted. "You care too much."

Paul nodded. "We just wanna take a look and keep brainstorming ideas. I think Bill and I work well together. Besides, it would give me another reason to make Gloucester my home." Paul smiled and winked at Carla. "Not that I really need another."

Now it was Carla's turn to blush. "So, what kind of ideas are you guys talking about? We already have deep sea fishing and tour boats."

"You're right," Paul replied, "And that's why we hope to find that little extra that might really go over with tourists as well as the locals. I mean, we still think we could rent it out for private parties and weddings, but we're kicking around the idea of making it educational somehow. Offering classes to schools on sea life, or the lobster industry."

"I don't know guys. That's sounds kind of boring."

"Says the girl who hated school," Bill said with a grin. "But what do you think about doing some painting parties around the harbor? It was Paul's idea, but I think it's brilliant with Rocky Neck bringing all the tourists every year."

"If you can figure out how to keep the easels from falling over when the boat rocks, that might be really cool," Carla mused. "You know what else might go over? A photography tour – between the landscapes from sea and some of the wildlife, that might be another whole audience."

"That's an awesome idea!" Paul gave her a kiss before turning to Bill. "I'm getting kind of stoked about this idea – not gonna lie."

"Me, too," Bill replied. "To be able to be out on the water every day, but not for twelve hours of lugging or navigating bad weather? I don't wanna be another Nate someday – he's almost a prisoner of the sea."

"Don't use that in your marketing campaign," Carla said, sliding off the stool. "You'd piss off every fisherman in the harbor."

Paul chuckled. "Right now, he's only worried about Nate. Am I right?"

Bill nodded. "Yeah, I'm not sure how to even bring up the topic with him."

"Then don't," Carla advised. "It's way too early in the game to worry about yet. So, when are you guys going to look at the boat?"

"Any time. You wanna tag along?"

*Oh, that damn smile gets me every time. Yeah, I'd love to tag along – but down on the docks we might run into some guys from my past days, and I'd hate for you to find out what a cheap tramp I was with so many of them.* She swallowed her fears and pasted on a smile. "No, you guys should go on your own. Besides, at some point I gotta head home and do some laundry."

Paul leaned in and kissed her cheek whispering in her ear. "Any chance I can come by later to tell you all about it? I can bring pizza."

"How about I cook dinner instead?" Carla murmured.

His grin set off all kinds of flutters inside her stomach. "Sounds great. I'll call you later when I'm on my way." He drank the last swig of his beer, and pushed his stool in.

"Ready?" he asked Bill.

"Yeah, let's go do this. Carla, good seeing ya. I have a feeling we might be seeing a lot more of each other if things work out. Tell Joey thanks for the beer."

Carla kissed Paul good bye and waved as they walked out together. *Damn, that man makes me so friggin' horny. And somehow, I have a feeling tonight might be the night. So why does that scare the hell out of me?*

She hung around the bar for another hour, helping Joey by taking inventory and putting in an order for the following Monday before wrapping utensils in napkins. He finally came out of the kitchen and shook his head. "Much as I love having you here, Squirt, it *is* your day off. Why don't you get out of here? I think Paul calmed you down better than I ever could."

Carla chuckled. *If you only knew, Joey. Right about now he's got me feeling anything but calm.* "I guess you're right. I do have some cooking and cleaning to do. See ya Monday."

She stopped at the store and picked up a small steak, along with everything else she'd need for fajitas and a salad. On impulse, she grabbed a small container of frozen creampuffs for dessert if she needed it. *Dessert...yeah, I can think of something I'd rather have for dessert. Jeez, why can't I get that man out of my head?*

Once home, she started in Nonna's bedroom, stripping the bed and changing the sheets, and then dusting and vacuuming the entire house. She wiped down the bathroom, which didn't need much more as she kept that clean on a regular basis, and then got dinner prepped before hopping in the shower and getting dressed.

*Why am I so damn nervous? It's not like I haven't done this more times than I can count.* As she was checking her reflection in the mirror, it dawned on her. *This is the first time with someone I really care about. What if it doesn't go well, or he finds out what a whore I was for so long? Or worse yet, what if all those times screwed up any chance of sex being special for me? Shit. Now I'm even more nervous.*

Carla drank a half a glass of wine to settle herself down as she sauteed the beef and onions, and the food was ready when he rang the bell.

Paul was dressed in jeans with a tee shirt peeking out from under a light weight sweater. She invited him in, and he pulled her in for a warm kiss that both calmed her nerves and flamed the desire that had been there all day. "Hmm...you smell like coconut," he murmured into her hair. Lifting his head, he grinned at her. "Which is almost as good as the smells in the kitchen."

"I kept it simple with fajitas and salad. Come on, it's all set."

"My stomach is growling," Paul said, following her into the kitchen. "Can I help?"

She retrieved a pot holder from the drawer. "If you wanna grab something to drink, help yourself to anything in the fridge."

Paul noticed her empty glass. "Looks like you've had wine. Want a refill?"

She nodded, watching his hands as he poured. *Concentrate, damn it, and get this meal on the table before you lose it!*

"What else do you need?" Paul asked.

*Oh, you have no idea, pal.* "I think we're good. Check the table to see if there's anything missing."

"Tortillas, sour cream, cheese, and salsa...I'd say you've thought of everything." He winked as he sat down. "At least for right now."

His smile melted something deep inside of her. *I don't know if I'm being stupid, but there's no way you're leaving here tonight, pal.* She placed the pan of fajita mix between them. "Help yourself. And hey, how did it go looking at the boat?"

"Not sure. It needs some structural work, which we're a little nervous about."

"Any other buyers?"

"Not yet, which gives us time to talk about what renovations might cost."

"I can tell you're stoked about it." *Almost as stoked as I am thinking about you staying over.* Despite the unspoken sexual tension between them, she relaxed and chatted throughout dinner.

Paul was the first to wipe his mouth and push his plate back. "This was awesome; almost as good as the company."

"If Nonna taught me one real skill, it was how to cook. Of course, the first time I wanted to make something Mexican, I had to listen to her swear at me in Italian for ten minutes." Carla smiled, wistfully remembering Nonna in the kitchen.

"You miss her?"

Carla nodded. "Comes in waves. One day I start crying when I pull out her favorite wooden spoon, and another I'll sit here and talk to her while I'm eating dinner. Grief is kind of weird."

"So...do you talk to her about me?"

"Nope, not a single time," Carla teased. "Of course, I tell her about you. She would have loved getting to know you."

"I would have liked that as well. Instead, I'll have to rely on your stories of growing up with her. You can start while I wash the dishes."

"You're gonna what?"

Paul pulled a towel off a hook by the sink and threw it at her. "Only if you dry – after you put the food away. Be done in no time."

Carla smiled. "A man that does dishes? Damn, how did I get so lucky?"

"I don't know, lady," Paul replied, pulling his sleeves up slowly, his eyes on Carla the entire time. "Somehow I feel like I might be the lucky one tonight."

She could only hold his gaze for a moment before feeling her cheeks flush, and she retrieved the plastic wrap for the leftovers. She worked next to him, occasionally feeling a jolt when his hand touched hers over the drying rack. By the time he rinsed the last item, her mouth was dry and her stomach was in knots with anticipation.

Paul stepped closer, taking the dish towel from her and hanging it up as his eyes held her gaze. "I think I'm ready for dessert now." His voice was husky as his lips found hers. Carla shivered as they connected, focusing only on his touch, his scent, and the exploding desire she'd never felt with anyone else.

"Are you sure you're ready?" Paul whispered. "I don't want to rush—"

She kissed him again, letting the last of her doubts and fears melt away. Taking his hand, she led him down the hall, past her old room full of heartbroken memories, to her new bedroom, full of the promise of new love and Nonna's blessings.

# CHAPTER THIRTEEN

Carla woke up to find Paul facing her, one arm bent to prop up his head. Paul reached out to tuck a loose curl behind her ear with his free arm. "Good morning, sleepy head."

"Have you been just lying there, watching me sleep?"

He stroked her cheek with his thumb. "Can't think of a better way to start my day. You're so damn beautiful with the morning sun streaming in on your hair." Laying back, he

held out his arm, inviting her to lay her head on his chest.

She caressed his skin with her finger, listening to his steady heart beat and stretching her legs out down next to his. *So, this is what it's like to wake up with someone. God, I don't ever want this moment to end. I feel so... safe. And at the same time, scared it will never last.*

Paul stroked her hair with one hand and cupped his other hand over hers, pulling her hand up to her lips to kiss each finger-tip. "I hope you slept as well as I did. I've thought of having you in my arms for a long time."

"Took me awhile to fall asleep."

"Hope I didn't snore."

"No...it's not...that," Carla stammered.

He lifted her chin up to meet his gaze. "You don't have any regrets, I hope – about last night."

"God, no," she assured. "Last night was…more than I ever dreamed it could be."

Paul's smile lit up his face. "Good to hear – and quite mutual, I might add."

Carla pulled back, lying propped up on her elbow. "I have something I have to tell you – and I hope it doesn't change anything between us."

"Honey, what is it? You look scared."

"Look, I know I told you I sort of had a…past…with guys," she started, "But I've never spent an entire night with any of them, and I'm feeling weird right now – like I don't how to act….I don't wanna screw this up, ya know?" She flopped down on her pillow and closed her eyes. "Maybe I just did by telling you all that." She didn't move, afraid to open her eyes, half expecting to hear him slipping out of bed to get dressed and run away.

Instead, she felt him moving closer, and felt his thumb caressing her lips and cheek as his breath warmed her face as he spoke. "Do you mean that I'm the first one to see you wake up in the morning?"

She opened her eyes to his face smiling down on hers. She nodded, and his smile got brighter. "Listen," he whispered. "You know I work down on the docks, and I've heard plenty about your…past. But to know that none of them ever got to hold you through the night, or see your beautiful eyes in the morning? God, am I lucky."

"I think I'm the lucky one," Carla whispered.

"And as for all those ghosts of your past, I know a way to put them to rest, once and for all."

"Hmm?"

He grinned, yanking the sheet down over her breasts and his own body until they were both naked in the sunlight. "I think it's time you had your first proper good morning." He pulled her close, kissing her lips, her face, and then the rest of her.

Carla let go of all inhibitions, giving herself in broad daylight to the man who made her feel loved and wanted for the first time. After years of wanting to run, she was finally home – right where she wanted to be.

Paul stayed the entire day, and Carla relaxed more and more as he made breakfast, washed dishes, and yelled as loud as she did when the Patriots game came on in the afternoon.

"So, you're a Pats fan, too? Something new I've learned about you today. How come it took so long?"

Paul munched on a cold fajita with leftovers from the night before. "You work a lot of Sundays, and then with the funeral and everything, I think our schedules were out of whack. Besides, I'm usually at Bill's to watch – he's a die-hard fan."

"Don't I know it. I grew up with those guys, remember? But hey, you gotta go over to Nate and Terri's place for a game sometime. Their basement's like a shrine -- unbelievable. Terri's been a huge fan all her life, and a lot of the kids in the Fort would pile into their basement for games. Good times – and tons of screaming."

"Good to know; maybe I'll mention it to Bill and we can watch the game with Nate sometime."

"Oh, he'll watch – but he could take it or leave it. He only watches cause his wife would leave him if he didn't."

Paul grinned. "Well, I'm glad to know that you and I will never fight over whether to watch the game or not. You might have yourself a permanent Pats buddy, Squirt."

Carla didn't reply, her attention on the television and a huge play. "Yeah! Third down conversion, baby!" She reached across Paul's lap for the bag of tortillas. "I think I could eat another fajita."

Paul held the bag up over his head. "Nope. No eating when they get inside the twenty. It's a choking hazard. Besides, it's just about halftime."

Carla was content to watch the last three minutes of the half; when the teams trotted off the field, she reached again for the bag, only to find it still out of reach. "Hey, what now? It's halftime!" She stood up to grab it out of his hands, but he placed the bag on the far end of the couch as he pulled her down on his lap.

"Exactly," Paul whispered, his breath warm on her cheeks. "It's time for our own little intermission. You game?"

Carla's body tingled all over as she understood his intent. "Oh, hell yeah..." She wrapped her arms around his neck and kissed him hard as he stood up and carried her down the hall.

By the time they emerged, the game was down to the last ten minutes, and they munched on another cold fajita as they watched the Pats win another. "I'm still hungry," Carla said, patting her stomach as the post-game show ended.

"Almost like you've worked up an appetite since I got here," Paul teased, handing her the last tortilla from the bag. "Finish it off, and I'll work on the rest of the chips and salsa."

They munched in silence as the evening game started, and Carla clicked the remote to turn off the television. "Unless you're into another game."

"Nope – I'm a loyal Pats fan to the end. Besides, much as I hate the idea of leaving, I *am* gonna have to go home at some point."

Carla sighed. "I kind of figured. But I'm really glad you stayed all day; this has been the best twenty four hours of my life, I think."

"Me, too. Hell, I'd ask to stay over again, but I'm not exactly dressed for work."

He picked up the empty dishes and took them into the kitchen and put them on the counter. As Carla joined him, he wrapped his arms around her and pulled her in for one last kiss. "I could get used to this – being here with you all the time. No rush, but any time you're lonely, I'm only a text away, ya hear?"

She nodded, gazing into his eyes and never wanting to look away. "I'll try not to text before you get out of the driveway."

"I'll call you tomorrow; can I...come by again when you get done at work?"

"On one condition," Carla teased. "Only if you bring whatever you'll need for Tuesday."

Paul kissed her hard, finally pulling away and picking up his keys to leave. "I'll pack an overnight bag as soon as I get home. See you tomorrow, Squirt. God, you're amazing..."

Carla watched him drive off before closing the door. *Talk about amazing. I already want you back here.* She almost danced through the living room, leaving the dishes in the sink as she ventured back to her new bedroom. She sat up, curling back into all the pillows except one, which she held in front of her as she slowly breathed in his lingering scent. *So, this is what it's supposed to feel like. Like you can't get them out of your head, and you don't want to try. I'm falling in love with him, Nonna – just like that. No one has ever made me feel this way before, and I can't wait until he's back here tomorrow. I hope you don't mind that I've taken this as my new room; somehow I feel like you're fine with it. You always wanted me to feel like Gloucester was home, and not a place to run away from. And Nonna, aside from maybe visiting my dad up in Nova Scotia, I think I'd be content to never leave this room again if Paul were here with me.*

# CHAPTER FOURTEEN

Betty Sue had survived her confrontation with Carla with the help of her friends. Sharon had listened to her wail for hours, and eventually Kelly joined them and they ordered take out rather than going out as planned. After Betty Sue went to bed and fell asleep, Kelly called the rest of the brunch club and filled them in.

All arrived Sunday morning for a potluck brunch except Arlene and Terri, who were at church. When Betty Sue exited her bedroom, she found Sharon, Kelly, Jean, and Peg sipping Bloody Marys and laying out serving dishes filled with eggs, sausage, croissants, and fruit.

Kelly spotted her first. "Morning, sleepy head. Glad you finally got some rest."

Betty Sue wrapped her robe tighter and tied it. "Oh, my heavens, I can't believe you all came here to be with me. I must look a fright after all that crying last night!"

Jean held up a drink. "Drink this. And don't worry about how you look; friends don't judge."

"Besides," Peg said, "We're all one Bloody Mary ahead of you – on an empty stomach, I might add." She picked up an empty plate from the stack on the counter. "I'm assuming we can finally dig in? I'm starving."

Sharon wrapped her arm around Betty Sue's shoulder. "Kelly and I thought you might need some support today, so she called everyone last night and had us all bring something for the table. I suspect you could use a little food before drinking too much of that."

"Oh, don't you worry your pretty little head about me – I'm not sure I could eat a thing right now. You go on, though..."

Kelly handed her a plate with a croissant and a spoonful of eggs. "You don't get anything else from the pitcher until this plate is empty, got it?"

Jean patted a seat next to her on the couch. "Come on, sit and nibble a bit. Sharon filled us in on what happened yesterday."

Betty Sue curled up on the couch as memories came flooding back. "I'm surprised the pillow isn't still wet. It was horrible – I think I've lost any chance of ever having a daughter again."

"Sounds like Carla sort of exploded," Peg said, scooping another piece of sausage off her plate.

"I deserved it...all of it." Betty Sue whispered. "She read some of Mother's letter word for word, and now she knows exactly how things happened. She'll never forgive me...not now."

"People forgive far worse crimes over time," Jean pointed out. "And I'm sure Carla wasn't thinking super rationally when she showed up here."

"I was scared she might hurt me. Can't say I'd blame her..." Tears welled up as Betty Sue placed her plate on the coffee table. "Last night I realized what a horrible mother I've been all these years. Not to mention a terrible daughter as well."

Jean reached out and squeezed her friend's hand. "Honey, it always hurts when we have to face parts of ourselves we've been avoiding. But maybe now you can finally heal and move for—"

"No, I'll never heal from this!" Betty Sue cried. She sipped her drink and shivered. "I finally see myself for who I am – maybe for the first time in my life. And it sucks."

"I think this is the first time I've ever heard you admit guilt or remorse," Sharon said.

"Ouch! The first time?" Betty Sue drank some more. "Now I feel even worse."

"Don't overdo it," Kelly suggested. "It comes across as insincere. But after hearing you last night and today, I agree with Sharon. You seem different. More self-aware. I kinda like this version of you."

"A lot of good it'll do me. I'll never be able to make amends to either of them. Mother *died,* and Carla will never speak to me again."

"I don't believe that," Sharon said. "Look at me. I was estranged from my family for decades – and then out of the blue, I find out my father wants to see me again."

"That's different," Betty Sue replied. "Your son helped mediate that reunion. I don't have anyone to—"

"Excuse me?" Peg said. "What the hell are we? Chopped liver?"

"She's right," Jean added. "Haven't we had your back since we were running around as kids on Pavilion Beach?"

Kelly nodded. "Even when you left us all to marry your Prince Charming, didn't we still stay in touch the whole time you lived down south?"

Betty Sue looked at each of them – the friends who had been there all her life – no matter what she did or how she ignored them, they never abandoned her. "Sometimes I wonder why you put up with me all these years. I haven't exactly been a great friend, either."

"Hey, we all come with baggage," Sharon said. "But I can tell you, the first time I met all of you this past summer, I was so envious. To have lifelong friendships that never die? Do you know what a gift that is?"

"Well, you're one of us now," Betty Sue replied. "And maybe someday I can be worthy of the friendship you've all given so freely over the years...Lord knows I'll never be able to make my daughter change her mind."

"You can't *make* her forgive you," Kelly pointed out. "You have no control over what Carla does, my dear – you can only worry about yourself and hope she comes around."

"But how will I *do* that? I don't know how to be alone. I never have."

"You've been on your own for years since Kenneth died," Kelly replied. "Even moving home, you didn't spend any more time with your mother than you had to – you've been living here alone all that time and doing just fine."

"Fine?" Betty Sue argued. "You call the whole Sean McClean affair fine? If it hadn't been for Sharon knowing who he was, he'd probably be out of the country with all my money by now. And I'd be right back where I started from in this town. Broke and alone."

"Sounds to me like you've been equating love with money all your life," Peg said. "But in the end, where has that gotten you?"

"How can you say that?" Betty Sue spat out. "After I've lost so much. My money is all I have to count on right now – and I've been quite happy over the years because of it."

"You believe that?" Peg didn't back down. "You couldn't wait to leave town when a man promised you a life of luxury, but did it really bring you happiness? Because I don't see it. Were you rich? Absolutely. But happy? I'm not sure you've ever found that -- and you know why? Because it was right here in the Fort the entire time you were gone. You just never saw it, because you always wanted what you didn't have."

"That's not fair!" Betty Sue curled up and grabbed the same pillow she had held onto when Carla was yelling at her. Tears welled up in her eyes, and she waited to have one of the others defend her. Instead, they all remained silent, waiting for Peg's words to finally settle.

Jean handed her another Bloody Mary. "Truth hurts, doesn't it?"

Betty Sue sniffled and nodded as she took a sip. "How come all of you figured it out way back then, and I never did?"

Jean settled in next to her. "I think we all had a sense of what we wanted to accomplish in life instead of the material things. I think your biggest issue is you've never figured out what your real purpose is."

Betty Sue sat quietly, trying to absorb yet another epiphany. "Well... I try to be nice to my friends...does that count?"

"She's right," Peg chimed in. "You really don't know what you want to be when you grow up, do you?"

"I'd say it's a little late for that, don't you think?"

"It's never too late to find your purpose," Sharon said. "Think back to when you were little – what did you want?"

Betty Sue's voice was almost a whisper. "All I ever wanted was for my mother to love me enough to give me time...but she was always too busy working so she could feed me. So, I decided I needed someone rich enough to give me time and money – like those two things were the same as happiness." She swallowed hard as tears filled her eyes. "I haven't got the slightest idea what my purpose is – I don't think I have one!"

Kelly leaned forward, excited for her friend's continued self-discovery. "Sweetie, don't you see? Now, you can figure that out, and concentrate on what makes *you* happy – without the need for anyone else giving you anything."

"She's right," Sharon added. "And until you do, you'll never be totally happy on your own. So again, what makes you happy?"

Betty Sue's mind was reeling, trying to look at herself through new eyes. "I have no idea – aside from taking my friends out for brunch or buying you things that made you smile, I just don't know."

"Bingo!" Kelly said. "You *do* have a purpose! You're right about being generous with us. You're genuinely happy when you have all of us over for brunch, or hear one of us talking about something we saw but can't afford, and then you'd buy it for us for our birthday or Christmas. Don't you see? Your *money* is the way you can help others!"

Betty Sue leaned back in her seat looking like a deer in the headlights. "But...I don't *want* to give all my money away. You saw how Sean almost destroyed—"

"Relax, sweetie. I'm not talking about all of it. I'm talking about investing some of it –maybe in a foundation or something -- and then those assets help others."

"She's right," Jean said. "Let's face it – you certainly have enough in the bank to give *some* of it away."

Sharon nodded. "It's a great idea. You'd be providing a financial boost – maybe to women who need it so they can make it on their own, and don't have to chase after a Prince Charming. Sort of a financial fairy godmother."

Betty Sue's eyes lit up with that image. "Why...I love fairy godmothers. That's what I always prayed for when I was a little girl... and I assumed she sent me Kenneth. But for me to be someone *else's* fairy godmother? I think I'd like to do that – or at least find out *how* to do that."

Kelly smiled. "My friend Debra knows someone at the Chamber of Commerce who's all about economic development in this town, and I think she'd be a great person for you to meet with, along with your banker – I know he's on the ball with your investments."

"Oh, he is. He's the one that noticed all the transfers from my accounts when Sean was trying to steal from me. I totally trust him with my money."

"Let me call Debra and have her set up a meeting; I'll go with you if you'd like. I might even get involved if the stakes aren't too high. I'd like to give back a little to the community that's been so good to me."

"I have another idea in the meantime," Jean said. "It might be a little trickier to pull off, but man, what a difference it would make..."

"What is it?" Betty Sue asked.

"It's Terri – and she'd kill me if she knew I was telling you this. You all know she's been doing physical therapy, but she's only doing another session or two because they can't afford it."

"But that's crazy! She needs it!" Kelly said.

"But they don't have insurance, and Nate's not taking the boat out as much anymore."

"Yeah, he was looking shaky at the funeral," Peg said. "I was wondering about his health."

Jean nodded. "Terri's worried about him. And you know her – she'll play the martyr if money is tight."

"But why hasn't she said anything? I'd be happy to help her and Nate."

"Are you kidding? Terri would never take a hand out – not even from friends."

"Peg's right," Jean said. "She told me the same thing. But I think it's possible to call the business office at the hospital and offer to pay someone's medical bills anonymously."

Betty Sue's eyes lit up. "Like a *secret* fairy godmother! I think I'd like to do that!"

Kelly grinned. "I think it's a great idea. Granted, I'd still love for you to meet my friend, but helping Terri's like a trial run to see how it makes you feel."

"Look at you, being all civic-minded," Sharon added. "Who knew I was staying next door to a philanthropist? I have a good feeling for you, Betty Sue. It might be exactly what you need."

"I'm actually excited to try this," Betty Sue said. "Thank you—all of you—for helping me figure it out. I really am blessed to have such good friends."

Peg held up her glass. "To Gloucester's newest fairy godmother – viva!"

# CHAPTER FIFTEEN

Terri's physical therapy was slowly helping, and having Hannah drive her back and forth and help around the house made a huge difference in her ability to function. She had managed to get her own shoes on, make the bed, and throw a meal into the crockpot before Hannah arrived.

"Look at you!" Hannah beamed. "You'll be firing me in no time. I hope you didn't push yourself too hard before therapy."

"Gotta push at some point," Terri replied. "Or I'll never get better. And I have to, it's that simple."

"Well, that's been the goal all along, and I'd say you're doing more and more each week." Hannah picked up the laundry basket. "I'll zip down and get this in, and then switch it over when we get back."

"Still not fast enough," Terri complained.

"What's the rush?"

"It's Nate. Something's not right with him – his hands have been shaky the last month or so. Bill said he's noticed it on the boat, too. I don't have time to deal with a damn back if he needs me to help more with the boat."

"Isn't Paul helping out now when he can?"

"Yeah, but they're only going out a few days a week – and between my PT bills, and a few doctor appointments I made for Nate, we may not be able to afford the extra set of hands – even if we need it."

Hannah got the laundry started and then helped Terri out to the car. "You guys don't have health insurance, do you?"

"Nope; not many fishermen do. That's why so many of the wives work in the processing factories; at least there's some basic benefits."

"So, when you had to give that up, you lost all the family benefits?"

Terri nodded. "We'll get by; that's what we do. And after this last round of sessions, I won't get any more. Can't afford 'em, and I can do the exercises at home. Hoping to be back driving in a couple of weeks, too."

"Trying to get rid of me, huh?" Hannah grinned.

Terri hesitated. "More like I really can't afford to pay you much longer – and you're already way underpaid as it is."

"You know I'd be happy to stay on for a bit even without pay. It's not like I have a lot of expenses living at home."

"We don't do charity – you know that."

Hannah drove the rest of the way in silence, wishing she could do more. Later on, she helped Terri back to the car. The older woman was sputtering and shaking her head.

"What's up with you? It must have been hard session," Hannah said.

"It's not that," Terri complained. "They told me I could keep coming for another three months – for nothing! I mean, what the hell?"

"Free therapy? And you're griping about it? Sounds like Christmas morning to me."

"That's not the point, and you know it," Terri argued. "And if your mother's behind—"

"I can guarantee you she's not," Hannah replied. "A teacher's pension is not a lot, and she doesn't make a whole lot on her art."

"They wouldn't tell me anything. And it bugs me."

"Not to be disrespectful, but maybe someone wanted to help without hurting your pride."

Terri shook her head, muttering to herself while Hannah drove the short distance to the supermarket. "You sure you don't want to sit out here? I can run in and get the items on your list if you wanna rest."

"I'll be fine, if I take it slow."

*You're so damn proud. And fiercely independent. It's so hard for you to accept help.* "At least let me drop you off at the door, and then I'll go park."

With no argument, Hannah pulled up into the fire lane and put her flashers on for a second. As she hopped out of the car to come around to help Terri out, Vinny Rossi came out of the store pushing a small cart. "Hannah, how are you?" He stopped short when he realized who was opening the passenger side door. "Mom."

Terri caught her breath. She'd seen her son at the funeral, but hadn't approached him at all. Now, here he was, only a few feet away. "Vincent." She tried to hide the grimace as she tried to pull herself out of the car on her own.

"Watch your back," Hannah blurted out, passing by Vinny to extend an arm for Terri to lean on.

"Mom, are you okay?"

Terri noted the worried look on his face. "I'm fine. A touch of sciatica, that's all."

"Can I help? You know you can call me any time. Especially if you need help." Vinny's concern for his mom pushed away any apprehension he might feel about talking to her. "Even if...Dad still has issues with it."

Terri's resolve was weak without Nate there to provide a reason to stay detached. "Vincent...you know I can't. He wouldn't—"

"Wouldn't approve?" Vinny finished her sentence, exasperation in his tone. "Will he ever? Mom, I can't change who I am. And I never thought you'd turn your back on me just because of the Pope. Especially after Anthony..."

Terri met his gaze, wanting desperately to reach out and hug him, hating the creed that kept her from being able to love her son the way she wanted to. "It's not that easy, son..." Her voice cracked, and a sudden weakness swept over her, causing her to grab a stronger hold on Hannah.

"Jeez, Mom, let me help you," Vinny moved in to her other side, supporting her other arm as Hannah whispered a thank you. "Here, take my cart – it'll give you some support."

Terri wouldn't meet his gaze as he held her arm, but she willingly accepted the cart to lean on. "I'm...okay now. You can let go."

Hannah closed the door behind her. "Listen. Vinny's gonna stand here with you while I park the car—"

"There's no need! I'm fine!" Terri's voice couldn't mask the fear of being alone with her son.

Vinny gestured for Hannah to proceed. "She's right. Let me stay – it'll only take her a minute to park." He stood there awkwardly, trying to find words to break the tension between them.

"When did your back start up again?"

"A few weeks ago," Terri replied quietly. "It's more in the hip right now. Hannah's been driving me to therapy for a while. It's been helping."

"And...how's Dad? I wanted to talk to you at the funeral, but he seemed a little shaky on his feet, and I didn't wanna cause a scene in front of Carla and her mom."

"He's slowing down a bit."

"You must worry about him."

Terri almost grinned. "Part of my job, ain't it?"

"Mom...when he's out on the water...I know you hate to ask for help, but I'd be there in a heartbeat – you know that, right?"

Terri finally met his gaze. "I...do. And thanks."

Hannah approached in a hurry, wishing she could wave a magic wand to make the tension disappear between them. "You doing okay?" Turning to Vinny, she smiled sympathetically. "Thanks so much for waiting with her. And for the cart. Good seeing you, Vinny."

"You, too, Hannah. I'll just grab my bags." He reached out to touch his mom's arm, and was relieved to see that she didn't wince or pull away. "Mom, remember what I said, okay? Please let me help." He noted her slight nod as he grabbed his bags and paused before turning to cross the parking lot.

Terri watched him go, blinking hard to stop the tears.

"You okay?"

Exhaling slowly, Terri grasped the cart handle tightly. "I'll be fine. We only need a few things." She pushed the cart ahead of Hannah, determined not to let her emotions get the best of her.

When Terri got home, she made a sandwich and said she was going in to "rest" for a bit. Hannah suspected she needed some space, so she headed downstairs and moved the laundry over to the dryer. She cut up chicken breasts and potatoes to throw together a quick dinner that Terri could eat any time, and Nate could either warm up or eat cold when he got home. Once the meal was in the oven, she raided the veggie drawer in the fridge and tossed together a simple green salad. *That should be plenty for the two of them tonight, with leftovers for tomorrow.* Terri was still in her room when Hannah finished folding the laundry and covered up the finished meal. She left a note on the table, and said she'd be back in a couple of days. *I suspect you're in there hiding because you don't want to talk about seeing Vinny. You can play the stubborn Catholic all you want, lady, but your heart wants him back. And I'll do everything I can to help make that happen – for both of your sakes.*

Later that evening, she mentioned the encounter to her mom. "They really connected today – even if only for a minute or two. I hope she calls him."

Jean shook her head. "Unfortunately, it's a big jump from her connecting in a parking lot to picking up the phone and calling. I don't think she'd go behind Nate's back, no matter how much she wants Vinny in her life."

"Not just Nate; she doesn't wanna piss off the Pope, either."

"Don't be irreverent – you know how much her faith means to her."

"Sorry, but I hate seeing them kept apart by some outdated creed."

Jean chuckled. "Sometimes I wonder how you made it through school without offending all your Catholic classmates with your pagan sass. It's a wonder Terri puts up with you."

"That reminds me," Hannah said. "After therapy today, she told me they scheduled her for another three months – at no cost! It was driving her crazy."

Jean hid a smile. "It's almost like she has a fairy godmother."

"Oh my God, you didn't! She's gonna kill you if she find out you—"

Jean put her hands up. "It wasn't me. But I might have mentioned it to somebody else I know who has a whole lot of extra money sitting around..."

"No way! Betty Sue paid for it?"

"You didn't hear me say that, okay? And don't tell Carla. I'm not sure she'd understand, and her mother needs a little time to try out this new charitable way of living."

"Sounds like they're both beginning to grow a bit. Think there's a chance for them?"

Jean grinned. "With a fairy godmother? Impossible things can happen any day."

# CHAPTER SIXTEEN

Betty Sue met Kelly outside the Chamber of Commerce, dressed in a stylish suit with a lacy blouse underneath.

"Don't you look like the business woman?" Kelly teased. "Are you ready?"

"I think so; it's like embarking on a whole new life for myself, and it's both exciting and scary."

"Honey, you've been treating your friends for as long as you've had money," Kelly replied. "Use the same money to make a difference in our community, and you'll be a respected philanthropist."

She led the way inside, and the secretary led them into an office overlooking one of the wharfs. A thin woman with long curly hair extended her hand to Kelly. "Sara Morris; so happy to meet you. I've seen you at chamber events, and it's nice to put a name to the face. I was thrilled when Debra told me you wanted to come in to chat."

"She's raved about you for years," Kelly said. "And this is one of my dearest friends, Betty Sue Marino."

"Please, sit," Sara said, gesturing toward a small conference table. "I've heard you're a generous woman who's thinking of using your money to make life better for others – I like doing business with that kind of woman. Let me tell you a bit about our vision for local economic development, and an option you might be interested in." She slid them each a folder with material inside. "It's a local foundation we're just getting off the ground – you can read about it later, but can I explain how it works?"

Both women nodded, and over the next hour Sara laid out various ways in which they could get involved. Betty Sue listened intently, asking questions, and taking notes. Finally, she had a few question of her own.

"So, if I join the board of this foundation, and donate assets to help fund it, I'd then help in making decisions about who received assistance?"

"Along with the other board members. Most of the help is offered in business grants to women in the area. We recognize that in a small fishing community, women don't have a lot of options outside of the processing plants."

"Which is exactly why I'm interested. Maybe if I'd had other options, I wouldn't have felt the need to escape. I've done a lot of soul searching recently, and I think I made some bad choices back then."

"I might disagree," Kelly offered. "You can't go back and get a do-over, and the bottom line is, if you hadn't left and married Kenneth, you wouldn't be sitting here with money to give away, now would you?"

"An excellent perspective," Sara said. "And trust me, the lessons you've learned are already guiding you into the areas where your money will make a difference. I might suggest you take the folder and meet with your financial advisor to get his input." The intercom on her desk beeped, and after answering it, she closed her file. "I'm afraid I have another appointment to get to, but let's plan on meeting again soon. It was delightful meeting both of you."

The ladies walked out, and Betty Sue grabbed Kelly's arm. "I can't remember the last time I've been this excited about something. I feel like a whole new person is bubbling up inside of me."

Kelly chuckled. "Well, to quote a wise philanthropist I know, 'Don't you worry your pretty little head about that.' I happen to think this is going to be the new and greatly improved version of you, my dear. And to celebrate, I'm going to take you to lunch!"

Betty Sue invited the gang for brunch that weekend to fill them all in on her new purpose in life. She woke up early and set up a lavish display of mini quiches, pastries, fruit and cheese, and sliced ham. The last item on the list was a couple of pitchers of Bloody Marys, as well as wine for a second option.

When the doorbell rang, she welcomed Sharon in first, who looked around and shook her head in wonder. "You could hire yourself out as a caterer, lady. What a beautiful spread!"

"Aww, what a sweet thing to say," Betty Sue gushed. "Just that Southern hospitality I learned while entertaining all of Kenneth's business associates. I think serving brunch is still one of my favorite things in the world."

"What can I do to help?" Sharon asked. "Any last minute items?"

Betty Sue scanned the room quickly. "How about lighting one of those wonderful candles I bought down in Caldwell last year? They all smell so divine!"

"You won't get an argument out of me," Sharon said, using the lighter on the mantle to ignite the carrot cake scented candle. "Hmm….perfect smell for fall. Another few weeks and you'll have to switch over to the Christmas and winter scents."

"I may have you bring me a few more the next time you visit," Betty Sue replied.

The doorbell signaled another guest, and Jean and Terri arrived together. Within the next fifteen minutes, Kelly, Arlene, and Peg also showed up. Over the course of brunch, Betty Sue explained the new foundation and her role as a new board member.

"So, let me get this straight," Terri said in her gruff, down to earth manner. "You're gonna actually give your money away to strangers – just to help them out?"

Arlene looked at her hostess with admiration. "Serving others is what we're called to do, Betty Sue. It sounds like a wonderful idea."

Peg was also impressed. "I have to say, lady – maybe Sean screwing you over was a good thing. Sounds like you've really found your true self after that fiasco. I think it's an awesome idea. This town has plenty of little businesses that could use a financial boost. I'd love to do a story on it once you get the ball rolling. It would be good publicity."

"Excellent idea," Jean said, raising her glass. "I think it's time for a toast for this lady. Betty Sue, I suspect your mom's passing, and some of the events since then, have been a real catalyst for your growth. I think I speak for all of us when I applaud the changes in your disposition. And I'm convinced that Elena is looking down on you right now, and she's really proud of her daughter. Viva!"

Betty Sue shared an understanding look between Jean and Kelly. *Of course she's part of all this. Mother, if you're up there...can you watch over Carla and help us to reconnect some day? When I've grown enough to be someone she can finally look up to? In the meantime, I'm so grateful for these ladies, who have loved me at my worst, and will no doubt nurture me as I start this transformation.*

# CHAPTER SEVENTEEN

Jean and Hannah crossed the street early Sunday morning to help Carla begin to clean out some of Elena's things. Carla had coffee and cinnamon rolls waiting when they arrived, and a list of items to address.

"I'd like to pack her clothes first, and donate them somewhere," she said, pouring Jean coffee. "And you can take the art work home today as well." As she joined them at the table, she continued. "It's... not too early, is it? I don't want to disrespect Nonna at all, but I'm also kind of looking forward to doing a little renovating."

"Hey, it's your house now; you can do whatever you want with it," Hannah said, helping herself to a cinnamon roll. "And let's face it, the house *needs* your energy. 'Old Italian Grandma' isn't your style."

"She's right," Jean added. "And Nonna would give her blessings. I suspect a *lot* of stuff you'll decide not to keep. Pick out a few things you love, and those will keep her spirit in the house. One thing to consider before getting rid of too much is whether you're planning on staying here, or selling the house for money to pursue your dreams."

"It's weird. For years, all I wanted was to escape this town. But now...with Paul here, and inheriting the house, I sort of feel like I belong here."

"Besides," Hannah teased, "What the hell would Joey do without you? He was lost those few days you took off for the funeral. You really do keep the place running."

Carla couldn't hide her grin. "Yeah, much as I complain about it, I do love Joey and the regulars. It doesn't pay a lot, but the job is pretty easy. I'm not sure what else I'd even wanna do at this point."

"Trust your intuition," Hannah offered. "If you're meant to do something different, it'll show up when the time is right. Sort of like how Paul happened to end up in Gloucester right when your Nonna was leaving you. And hey, what about your dad? Have you thought about trying to find him?"

Carla licked the cinnamon roll icing off of her finger before answering. "I've thought about it. But then I wonder if things have changed over time. He wrote that letter a long time ago. He might have moved and gotten married and had a bunch of kids right now."

"Or," Jean countered, "He might still be in Nova Scotia and wondering about how life is for his little girl." She took a sip of coffee and met Carla's gaze. "Don't let fear keep you from reaching out – you might be pleasantly surprised."

"And worst case scenario?" Hannah asked. "You're no worse off than you are now. So, what's keeping you?"

Carla shrugged. "Oh, it's the fear, trust me. Right now, with the letter, I can tell myself he loved me. Do I wanna mess with that? If he's changed his mind, I'd go right back to feeling like I wasn't worth shit to either of my parents."

"Not necessarily," Jean said, taking her empty cup and plate to the sink, "You'll always know that he wanted you for quite some time...and that doesn't change even if *he* has." She retrieved the other empty plates from the table, leaving coffee mugs to be finished. "As for your *other* parent, one of these days we're gonna sit down and talk. Your mom's becoming a little more self-aware these days, and it's a good change for her. Maybe for both of you down the road."

"Yeah, right--like she'll ever change. I won't hold my breath waiting for *that* transformation. Besides, with Nonna gone, it's so peaceful not having Mom show up during the week."

Jean sat back down and reached out to take Carla's hand. "Much as I hate to bring this up, have you contacted her about items she might want?"

Carla pushed her hand away. "*Excuse* me?"

"She did grow up here – and lived here with you and Nonna for five years—"

"Before abandoning us for good!" Carla almost knocked her chair over as she got up and stormed to the sink with her empty cup. "I don't owe her a *damn* thing from this house!"

"No, you don't," Jean replied gently. "But that doesn't mean you shouldn't make the offer. Especially if you're going to throw a bunch of stuff into a dumpster. Some of it might have sentimental value for her."

"Sentimental value?" Carla spit out, grabbing a sponge and wiping the table vigorously. "Are you friggin' kidding? Fine--she can go dumpster diving if she wants something."

Hannah lifted her empty cup and giggled. "I'd almost pay money to watch your mom climbing into a dumpster."

Carla grinned, throwing the sponge back into the sink before sitting down. "I'll put her stuff on the bottom with a bag of garbage on top of it."

"Look, all I'm suggesting," Jean offered, "Is to let her know you're getting rid of stuff, and if she wanted to look through what you're throwing away, she might find something she'd like to keep – and now I won't mention her name again today, I promise."

"She has a point," Hannah added. "And it might result in a few less things to haul outside. In the meantime, I have an idea about your dad. Have you looked for him on social media?"

"You know I don't do any of that crap," Carla scoffed. "I don't need the world telling me what a mess I've made of my life. I do that just fine on my own."

Hannah laughed. "You might be surprised. There's one person who was kind of raving about you on his page last night."

"What do you mean?" Carla asked.

Hannah pulled out her phone and pushed some buttons, and held up a picture of Carla behind the bar at the Even Keel, with Joey's arm wrapped around her. The caption read *"We all knows who really runs this place. Glad to have her back."*

"*Joey* has a Facebook page?"

"Jeez, sometimes I think you're as old as Nonna when it comes to technology," Hannah teased. "And yes, Joey has a page – although he really *should* have one for work."

"Why? It's just a dive bar."

"Maybe now," Jean chimed in. "But back in its day, it was a local favorite. Joey's a great cook, and he could do more business with some advertising and a little sprucing up."

"I'm not sure Joey wants more business; I think he keeps it as a place to hang out."

Hannah pushed more buttons, and looked up to meet Carla's gaze. "Guess what else I found?"

"What?" Carla asked nonchalantly.

"I think it's your dad. It's a Brad Douglas, from Peggy's Cove." She paused, watching Carla's face tighten. "So...should I open it?"

Carla sat frozen for a moment, her mouth suddenly dry. Taking a deep breath, she nodded slightly as her pulse quickened.

Hannah pushed a final button, and slid the phone across the table.

Carla knew in an instant it was him; her breath caught in her throat as she realized just how much she looked like him. The dark curls, the square jaw, and bright smile. Tears filled her eyes as the eyes in the photo seemed to look directly at her. "It's...him. My dad." She swallowed hard, studying the man kneeling on the rocks with the ocean behind him and a brown cocker spaniel in his arms. "He...has a dog."

She held up the phone so Jean could take a look. "I guess we know who you take after; you look just like him."

Hannah agreed. "Ready to learn more?" When Carla nodded, she took the phone back and hit another button. "Says he's self-employed at Brad's Carpentry Shop, went to school at Gloucester High, and his birthday is in December, like yours. He's also listed as single, and has no family or relationship info listed."

"Sounds like he never remarried then," Jean said.

Hannah slid the phone back to Carla. "There's more photos..."

Carla swallowed hard, the lump still in her throat as she scrolled through numerous photos of her dad, mostly with his dog or in front of various boats or woodworking projects. "He made all these things himself? They're gorgeous." She slid the phone over for Jean to see. "But after all these years? I can't imagine he'd want to be bothered by me now."

Jean was scrolling through photos when one caught her eye. "Honey, I think you're wrong about that…I'm assuming this is his own boat. Look at the name."

Carla took the phone back and saw another shot of Brad with his dog, this time perched in the back area of a small sailboat. On the back, the detailing read *Carla's Dream.* This time tears spilled over. "He…named his boat…after me?" She leaned back in her chair sobbing, her eyes fixed on the smile that seemed to jump out of the photo in front of her.

Jean reached out and squeezed her hand. "I suspect he would love nothing more than having his little girl contact him after all these years."

Carla's sobs continued, and Hannah got up to grab a box of tissues from the counter. She placed it on the table and wrapped her arm around her best friend's shoulder. "Been an emotional roller coaster lately, hasn't it?"

Carla nodded, pulling a tissue out of the box and blowing her nose. "That's putting it mildly. I didn't know I had this many tears in me." She took a few deep breaths, once again picking up the phone to stare at the father she'd never known. "Do you really think he'd want to hear from me?"

"Jeez, he named his friggin' boat after you – I'd bet money on it."

"I don't know," Carla replied. "I don't think I could handle getting my hopes all up and then finding out I was wrong."

"I get that," Hannah said.

Jean offered a solution. "You *could* just send him a message and give him your email or phone number, and then it's up to him."

"Yeah, I guess…and if he didn't respond, I'd have my answer at least."

"But if he does," Hannah pointed out, "You'd maybe have your dad. I could even send it for you right now." She picked up her phone and met Carla's gaze. "Before you lose your nerve."

Carla wiped her tears with sweaty palms, her stomach churning inside. Afraid to speak, she gave a little nod as she stood up. "I'm gonna go start on Nonna's clothes."

Jean watched her almost race down the hall. "I think she needs a little time to process all this. Poor kid."

"So, do I send it? I have it all set to go – a simple message and her phone number."

"You might as well, although we don't have to tell her unless she asks. In the meantime, we can start on the closet in the living room and get all of Elena's coats and boots and purses out and into a bag."

Jean opened a bottom drawer and pulled out a few big garbage bags for clothing. Before she could hand one to Hannah, they both heard Carla's phone ringing from the bedroom and froze.

"Oh my God," Hannah whispered. "Do you think that's him calling already?"

"If it is, then all the more reason to stay out here. She'll come out when she's ready."

They worked together for the next thirty minutes, stopping every now and then to listen down the hall.

"She's still talking," Hannah whispered. "Maybe it was Paul calling."

"Or maybe she and her dad have a lot to talk about. Come one, let's keep busy."

They pulled out all of Elena's old belongings, along with a few items they weren't sure of. Hannah grabbed a dust pan and brush and cleaned up the floor, leaving only Carla's boots, winter coat, and a few sweatshirts still remaining. "She's got lots more storage room here – that's for sure."

By the time they were folding the last of Elena's things, Carla emerged from the back room. Her eyes were puffy from more tears, but her smile revealed that the call had been a good one.

"Was that him?" Hannah asked.

Carla nodded, her eyes misty with more tears. "He's coming down to visit. I'm gonna see my dad again after all these years!" Both Jean and Hannah encircled her with arms, crying tears of joy along with her.

Jean finally stepped back and gently wiped tears from Carla's face. "And you were afraid he wouldn't want you anymore…"

"He asked about everything," Carla said, her eyes lighting up. "What I did, and where I lived, and how Elena was…he was sad to hear about her, but glad I finally got the letter. Turns out, he assumed I didn't want anything to do with *him*. Said he tried to find me on social media and everything."

Hannah laughed. "Well, maybe *now* you'll have some motivation to finally join the modern age like the rest of us. I'm *so* happy for you!"

Jean agreed. "So, when's he arriving?"

"In a few weeks. He's even gonna bring Rufus along."

"Rufus?"

"His dog. 'Rufus the Doofus' is his full name – says he's really sweet and loving, but not very bright. He's gonna book a room at the Cape Ann Motor Inn – it's dog-friendly."

"Smart plan," Jean replied. "Not sure you'd want him here quite yet – even if you *do* have room."

"Yeah, I think the first day at least I need a neutral spot; I could always invite him here if things go well." Carla plopped down on the couch next to the plastic bags, noting the almost empty closet for the first time. "My God, did all this stuff come out of there?"

"Your grandmother had a lot of old purses and sweaters. I've gone through all the pockets, but you and Hannah can check all the purses. Elena used to carry an 'emergency ten' in her purse when I used to take her to appointments. You might get lucky."

After going through six old purses, Carla held fifty dollars in her hand. "Jeez, I wish I'd known about these all those times we were short on cash. I wonder if she has money stashed anywhere else?"

"Wouldn't surprise me," Jean said. "When my mom died, I found money in her underwear drawer, under the mattress, in her old crock pot, and under the dining room tablecloth. Several hundred dollars by the time I was finished."

Carla grinned. "Maybe Nonna's room has all kinds of hidden treasures. Still, I'll start on my old room, just in case my dad does end up staying here a bit."

"I have an idea." Hannah grabbed the money from Carla's hands. "What if we used this for paint and transformed your old room into a real guest room? Your dad could be the first one to use it." Her eyes twinkled. "I assume Paul sleeps *elsewhere* when he stays over."

Carla's face blushed as she took her money back. "You assume correctly. And I can't wait to introduce the two of them."

Jean picked up a bag and started for the door. "Then I suggest we get busy and clear some stuff out so you can start renovating this place into your own. And I'm so glad he's coming down to visit. I know Nonna's smiling right now."

# CHAPTER EIGHTEEN

A few weeks later, Carla stood holding Paul's hand in the gazebo at Stage Fort Park. Her heart was racing as her dad's arrival time approached. "I'm so friggin' nervous."

Paul squeezed her hand. "Take a deep breath, and listen to the surf. Guaranteed to calm you down."

She turned her attention toward the water. Outside the gazebo was a big patch of lawn where the locals would picnic or listen to the community band play concerts all summer, and beyond that, the sandy beach. She closed her eyes, following his suggestion, focusing on the sound of waves crashing and salt air filling her lungs. Her breathing slowed along with her heart rate.

"Better?"

"Hmm-hmm. For now, at least."

Paul pulled her close and kissed her hair. "He's gonna love you. How could he not?"

"What if I'm not what he expects?" Carla's voice was almost a whisper. "Then what?"

"Squirt, those are your nerves talkin', that's all. Just be you."

Carla wrapped her arms around Paul, burying her head into his flannel shirt and breathing in his musky scent. "What if I'm not good enough?"

Paul ran his fingers down her spine, feeling her shiver when he found the hollow of her lower back. "That should remind you how amazing you are." He stepped back, cupping her face with his hands. "Now stop doubting yourself. You've got this. And later on..." His lips found hers, and they kissed deeply. "You can tell me all about how wonderful he is."

Carla nodded, stepping back with a grin as her hand traced a path from his neck down to his belt. "Maybe not *right* away. But thanks for waiting with me for a bit." She scanned the parking lot. "I guess you better leave before he gets here. See you tonight."

"Can't wait." He kissed her deeply, pulling her close.

She watched him walk toward his car. *Even if he doesn't like me, I still have you. That'll make it okay.* Turning back to watch the waves brought her grandmother to mind. "Okay, Nonna, I know you're watching over me right now. Please let him love him."

She leaned against the railing of the gazebo, watching the waves to her left, and the parking lot to her right. The next few minutes dragged, and each time a car pulled in, the lump in her throat grew, until she spotted a cocker spaniel walk out from behind a truck. *Rufus. It has to be Rufus. Looks just like his photo.* As he sniffed the grass, Carla's heart raced when her dad came into view at the other end of the leash. She stood with sweaty palms, meeting his gaze. He let Rufus explore the new smells between them, but his eyes never left hers once he spotted her.

When they got within ten feet of the gazebo, Rufus, darted up the two short steps, tail wagging, to meet his new friend.

Carla finally faced her father, her eyes tearing up. "Hey..." Her voice cracked, and she turned her attention to the cocker spaniel eagerly sniffing her sneakers. She fell to her knees, needing a second to gain composure. "You must be Rufus." She welcomed his wet kisses and dancing paws against her sweatshirt. *I can do this.* She looked up at Brad, also with misty eyes and a gentle smile.

"You're so beautiful," he whispered, extending his hand and helping her up. He pulled her into a hug, tentatively at first, but then held her tight as he sobbed. She clung to him, trying not to cry, but joined him despite her resolve. With her hand pressed tight against his chest, she felt his heart pounding.

Brad let go first, stepping back to wipe his eyes. "I told myself I wasn't gonna lose it...I'm glad I'm not the only one."

Carla didn't even bother wiping her eyes. "I...never thought...but here you are..." She stepped back and swallowed hard. "I'm...so friggin' nervous."

"Me, too. I spent the whole ride practicing what I'd say, and now can't remember a damn thing."

Carla took a deep breath and stuck her hand out, hoping he wouldn't see it shaking. "Hi...I'm Carla...I'm glad you came."

Her dad gripped her hand and shook. "Brad...and there was no way in hell I wasn't coming down to see you." He grinned at his dog, who was engrossed by seagulls on the beach. "And you've met Rufus."

At the sound of his name, Rufus danced around Carla's feet. "I think he's given his approval."

"What a good boy," Carla murmured, scratching behind his ears. "He's a lovebug."

"Pretty much," Brad replied. "Tide's coming in. God, I've missed this place." He gestured down toward the water. "You up for a walk? I think Rufus would love to chase some seagulls and get covered with sand."

Carla nodded, and they left the gazebo, walking over the green grass toward the beach. Neither spoke until they reached the sand, and Brad kicked off his sandals. "Gotta feel the sand between my toes."

Carla reached down and removed her sneakers. Rufus immediately trotted down to the water, sniffing seaweed and barking at gulls along the way. "You can tell he's a beach dog."

"Every day – but he's curious about the new smells here." Brad took a few more steps before speaking. "This is weird for both of us. Am I right?"

"Oh, God, yeah. I mean, I know you're my *dad*, but..." She dropped her eyes, her mouth as dry as the sand she looked at. "It's like..."

"I'm more of a stranger?"

She nodded, grateful he had voiced the words she was afraid to say. "I'm not even sure what to call you – and I hate that." She finally found the courage to meet his gaze, and his smile reassured her.

Brad reached out to squeeze her hand. "It's okay to feel unsure. For both of us. How 'bout you call me Brad for now, and we start by simply getting to know each other?"

Carla's shoulders relaxed, and she grinned. "Good plan. Although I have a confession to make. My friend is on social media, so I've seen all your photos, and your shop, and your house..." She paused, remembering the one photo that had yanked at her heartstrings. "And your boat."

Brad nodded with understanding. "I hope that didn't bother you too much, naming my boat after you – it felt right at the time. Still does."

Carla smiled. "It's a beautiful boat, and that photo is why I contacted you. It meant..." Her voice trailed off and she dug in her pockets. "I think I need tissues this time."

"I've got more if you need more. Maybe we leave the heavy stuff for later, and focus on the little things to start?"

Carla tucked her tissue away. "Like what?"

"I don't know – favorite foods? Music? Colors? Things..." Brad's voice faltered, "...a father and daughter should know about each other."

"Pizza," Carla began, smiling at the phrase.

For the next half hour, they strolled through the incoming waves, laughing about both hating grapefruit, loving Bob Seger & The Doobie Brothers, and preferring dogs to cats. Rufus chased gulls, almost got pinched by a cantankerous crab, and proudly claimed an old frisbee left on the beach as his new favorite toy. When they got back to the gazebo, Rufus shook himself hard, sand flying everywhere, and rolled around in the grass.

"You were right about him getting covered in sand," Carla said.

"I keep a towel in the truck – and luckily he likes the outdoor shower I have at home to wash him off before tracking sand all over the house."

Carla leaned against the railing, breathing in the salt air. "So...can you tell me about Peggy's Cove, and how you ended up there?"

Brad's gaze shifted from a distant fishing boat on the horizon to his daughter. "I'll answer every question you throw at me – but how 'bout we grab ourselves a pizza and then find a picnic table down in the grove?"

"Now you're talking my language."

"I don't suppose Bruno's is still around?"

Carla grinned. "Jeez, how do you do that? I'm only in there like once a week getting dinner."

"You were stealing bits of their pepperoni pizza off my plate before you could walk...come on, you can ride along with Rufus and me, if you'd like."

She nodded, helping her dad to wipe down the cocker spaniel before climbing up into his truck. Brad reached behind his seat and gave her a clean towel. "He'll be on your lap, guaranteed. Hope you don't mind."

Carla welcomed the still damp mutt, accepting wet kisses in return for scratches behind the ears. *I can't believe I'm in my Dad's truck, holding his dog. It feels so right, so comfortable. Like there hasn't been twenty years between us.*

They kept conversation light until they were back at Stage Fort Park and started on their second slice of pizza. Gulls perched on rocks by the water, complaining that the meal wasn't being shared. Rufus sat watch, guarding his human's meal as the raucous cries continued.

Carla watched them and chuckled, and then spotted a man with his young daughter further down the grove playing catch.

Brad noticed her expression darken. "What's that look for?"

"So why didn't you fight for me?" Carla blurted out. "Why are we sitting here twenty years later catching up, when we could have had *that?*"

Brad glimpsed over at the duo playing, and grew silent. "I've been waiting for you to let loose – I actually thought you might start right in on me when I first showed up. You certainly have every right to be angry."

"Believe me," Carla retorted, "You'd know it if I was 'letting loose.' I swear like a sailor and throw things when I'm mad." Her voice grew quieter. "But you don't know that since you haven't been around." Her eyes grew misty as her gaze met his. "Do you have any idea how different my life might have been if you'd been here, or if you'd come to get me?"

Brad swallowed his pizza and flung one crust toward the gulls before giving the other to Rufus. "He'll be asleep as soon he finishes. As for your question, you have no idea how often I considered it. But you gotta understand – for a number of years, I was in no position to offer you anything."

"What do you mean?"

"I, ah, lost myself -- in a bottle of Canadian whiskey. A lot of bottles, actually. It...took me several years to admit I was an alcoholic – and another couple of years to sober up and start putting some kind of life together." His voice faltered as his eyes met hers. "By the time I was in a place where I could have been a real dad to you, I heard that your mom had met Ken and was gonna be getting married..." Brad shrugged, almost in defeat. "I figured it was too late. That's when I sent your Nonna the letter."

"I had no idea," Carla whispered. "About the drinking, I mean. You're okay now?""Been sober for twenty years. One night I saw your mom on TV; they were in Halifax for some big event and he was being interviewed on the news. I heard her laugh – that's what caught my attention – and there she was, standing next to him, looking just as gorgeous as she ever had. She looked so damn happy..." Brad's voice broke as he continued. "I picked up some whiskey on the way to an old houseboat I was staying on, and was ready to climb right back into that bottle." He sighed heavily. "I'm so grateful I didn't."

"What...stopped you?"

"You did," Brad croaked, tears filling his eyes. "I realized I'd lost your mom forever that night...and even though it helped to see her looking so happy, it still hurt like hell to know I'd never been able to make her feel that way. But before I could take a swig out of that bottle, I thought of you...held on to a shred of hope that maybe someday I'd hear from you, or get to see you again...so I did the only thing I could to keep that hope alive."

"What's that?"

"Threw the whole damn bottle overboard."

Carla chuckled. "Did you jump in after it?"

"Only thought about it for a second or two before deciding I'd never touch another drop. I wasn't sure how I'd manage, but I knew somewhere I had a kid who deserved more than a drunk bum for a dad." He reached out for her hand, hesitating until her hand found his. "I'm so sorry for all the time we lost out on."

Carla nodded and wiped her tears. "Me, too...but thanks for telling me what happened. Makes it a little easier to understand." For a few moments, they sat silent within their own thoughts, as the cries of the seagulls almost voiced the roiling emotions between them. She stared out at the horizon, unable to meet his gaze as she asked one more question. "When I found you on social media, there was no indication of you ever getting married again. What's up with that?"

Brad caressed the top of her hand, still in his, with his thumb. "I tried dating a couple of times, but I knew there was no use."

"How come?"

"Because I've never stopped loving your mom – I don't think I ever will."

Carla yanked her hand away from his. "How can you *say* that? You don't even *know* her anymore!"

"True," Brad replied. "But love's not easy to forget when you give your heart and soul to someone."

"Yeah? Well, neither is the pain when they rip it out and throw it away before abandoning you!"

"I'm so sorry she—"

"Don't you go apologizing for her!" Carla spat out. "She's had *years* to make amends since Ken died, but she's still just as self-centered as she ever was! I wish she had stayed in Tennessee!"

"She's...back?"

"Oh, *shit!*" Carla retorted, scaring Rufus awake and alert. "Leave it to mother to screw up a perfectly great day. Yeah, she's back − and since the asshole who was dating her to steal her money went to jail, she's been in her 'damsel in distress' mode. You'll have no trouble riding in to save the day − at least until she dumps you for the next guy that comes along." She crumbled up her plate and threw it in the trash can. "I gotta go. Paul's coming over tonight."

Brad stopped her, placing his hands firmly on her shoulders. "Hey, I drove down from Nova Scotia to see my *daughter.*" He gently lifted her chin with one hand until she couldn't avoid meeting his gaze. "I'm sorry my reaction hit a nerve. Honestly, I didn't come to see her − I didn't even know she was here."

"Yeah, well the way you lit up like a Christmas tree when you found out tells me it's just a question of time before you're knocking on her door. That's a reunion I can do without, so—"

"Stop." Brad put a finger to her lips. "The only reunion I care about right now is standing in front of me, so please let's not talk about your mother."

"But she always—"

"Shh...just you and me. I mean it."

Carla's shoulders relaxed and she almost smiled. "And maybe Rufus?"

"Hey, we're a package deal," Brad teased. "Look, this was the best day I've had since I left here, and I don't want anything to come between us getting to know each other. Just say you'll give us a chance." He held out his arms invitingly. "Please?"

Her hug was all the reply he needed.

# CHAPTER NINETEEN

Two days later, Carla woke up early and stopped by the Brine & Brew to pick up coffee and donuts. She had just placed her order when a familiar voice laughed behind her.

"Well, you're either really tired and hungry," Hannah teased, "Or you've got yourself a morning date. Paul?"

Carla grinned. "Nope, not today."

"Oh, my God – then it has to be——"

"He's still here, and it's been amazing!"

Hannah squealed and flung her arms around her best friend. "Oh, honey, I am SO happy for you. I know how much you wanted this to go well."

"I'm actually heading up to Long Beach to see if he'd like to stay at the house for the rest of his visit." She waited for Hannah to place order before continuing. "You don't think it's too soon, do you? It just feels right."

"Trust your gut. If it feels right, then it sounds like a great idea."

"By the way, I'm not the only one buying coffee for two – what's up?"

This time it was Hannah's turn to grin. "JJ's been studying like crazy for his GED, and he's taking all of them today; I'm gonna drive him down to Salem and hang out there for the day."

"You, in Salem? Talk about being in your element."

Hannah grinned. "Gotta recharge my witchy vibes. It'll be a good day for me; gonna spend some time figuring out where I go from here – Terri's only gonna need me for a little longer, and I'm not really sure what I wanna do."

Carla handed the cashier money. "You know exactly what you wanna do – you're just scared to take the leap."

"You know me too well."

"And don't you forget it. So, back to JJ -- I take it things are going well in that department?"

Hannah grabbed her order off the counter. "Let's just say it might be time for a double date before long…he and Paul are gonna have to like each other if they're dating us. Am I right?"

"Damn straight. And you have to meet Brad, too. I mean, he'll be right across the street for a bit – that is, if he agrees."

"I suspect he'll jump at the chance. Do you know how long he's staying?"

Carla grinned as they stepped out into the sunshine. "He'll be here another week – maybe longer, depending on when supplies were due in for a job back home. I'm trying not to think about it – you know I don't do well with people leaving."

"Maybe Nonna left to make sure Paul and Brad stick around – that's my theory, anyway."

"From your mouth to Nonna's ears – I know she's got a good connection with the guy upstairs."

They reached Hannah's car first, and Carla waited until her friend was set before saying goodbye. "Tell JJ good luck from me – and maybe later on you'll see a strange truck in my driveway."

"Here's hoping – see ya, bestie!"

*Here's hoping for sure.* Carla crossed the street and looked out on the harbor before getting into her car. *And Nonna, I know it's been a long time since he was at the house, and the memories might not be so good. If Hannah's right, can you help him feel welcome?* With resolve, she buckled her seat belt and headed north toward Long Beach.

She spotted his truck in the lot when she arrived, and pulled in next to it. She counted six other cars as she got out and locked the door. *I love off season; after being packed all summer, we finally have the beaches back to enjoy until next spring.* She walked around to the front of the building, breathing salty air as the waves crashed about two hundred feet away. *Tide's just about in – and I don't see him out on the beach, so he must be inside.* A dog's water dish outside one of the ground floor sliding doors verified the room number Brad had given, and she heard Rufus bark when she knocked on the glass.

A black nose and two front paws greeted her before Brad had the door open, and she handed him the bag and cardboard coffee holder to allow for wet morning kisses. "Good morning, handsome," she whispered, reaching into her pocket to pull out a dog bone treat. "I brought you breakfast."

"You spoil him," Brad laughed. "He might wanna stay with you when it's time for me to head north. So, what's smells so good in here?" He opened the bag to find two huge frosted cinnamon rolls.

"One of those is mine – and I know this place has plates in the cabinet." She passed by Brad and retrieved two plates and two forks, returning to join him at a small table.

He opened the drapes to provide morning sun and the foamy surf as amenities. "So, I take it you've been here before, then. You and Paul? Or maybe an old beau I don't know about?"

"Hardly." The sweetness of the cinnamon roll waned as Carla remembered the night in question.

"I get the feeling it's not a good memory – you don't have to talk about it."

"It's okay." Carla leaned back, lingering over her coffee before answering. "It was supposed to be a nice romantic evening; I had saved up to reserve a room so we could stay over and wake up tangled in the sheets like they do in the Hallmark movies."

"I take it that didn't happen?"

"There was a guy I really liked in high school, but he only had eyes for my best friend. And then he left for years, and this past year he came back, looking hotter than ever..." She sighed, shaking her head. "But when I asked him if he wanted to hang out, he told me he was still only interested in one person...so I hooked up with some jerk who was working a boat in port for a couple of days. I just needed a break from Nonna that night..."

Brad reached out and placed his hand over hers. "And you brought him here for the night."

Carla swallowed hard, unable to meet her father's gaze. "That was the plan...I don't think he was here for more than an hour. After he got what he came for, he grabbed a couple of slices of pizza on his way out."

"Oh, sweetie, I wish—"

"It's okay. I took a long walk on the beach, cried myself to sleep, and then ate some cold pizza on my way home early the next morning. I shouldn't have left Nonna..."

"Something happen?"

"I walked in to find my neighbors cleaning up the kitchen, and found out Nonna had walked out in her night gown, leaving the burner on with a pot holder just inches away...God, it was the worst day of my life besides...losing her for good."

"She was a strong lady. I remember her laughing and telling stories – mostly about the fish factory." For a moment, only the raucous cries of the gulls amid the surf were heard. "You really miss her, don't ya?"

"I do. But I know she's watching over me, and I still believe she had something to do with Paul coming to town...and...you."

"I wish I would have known more about what was happening; I would have come back a long time ago if I did." He nudged her hand toward the cinnamon roll. "And I'm sorry I interrupted a really delicious breakfast...go on, eat up a bit."

Carla gave a soft smile before taking another bite. "I guess all that really matters is that you're here now."

"I'd still like to try and make up for some of the time we've missed."

"I, ah....have an idea about that." His silent response invited her to continue. "You don't have to, but I was wondering if…" Carla locked her gaze on the sticky pastry crumbs on her plate, afraid to look at him. "Maybe you might think about staying with me for the rest of your visit?"

She didn't expect the broad smile and twinkling eyes. "At the house? You'd really let me come and stay with you?"

"I think I'd really like you there."

"Well then," Brad replied, "You finish that breakfast of yours, and I'm gonna straighten up and pack my bag so we can get outta here."

"Can I ask one thing before we leave?"

Brad lifted his travel bag onto the bed. "Name it," he said, unzipping the top.

"Do you think we could take Rufus for a walk on the beach? I remember how nervous I was the day you arrived, and that walk on the beach felt…"

"Almost normal?"

Carla nodded, grateful he had found the words she was struggling to express.

Brad grabbed clothes, toiletries, and books, all the while sharing his favorite anecdotes from their first day together. Rufus followed him back and forth, wagging his tail, sensing a new adventure. Carla finished her cinnamon roll and coffee, offering the last bite to Rufus, who licked her hand and rolled over for a belly rub.

"Are you all excited about going out to play in the sand?"

"I'll make sure we clean him off real good before getting your house all dirty." As he zipped up his bag, Brad added, "And I could pick up a crate for him if you want; he's really well behaved, but I don't want him to mess up your house if you're not used to pets."

Carla scratched behind the dog's ears. "There's nothing in the house he can ruin, trust me. He can climb up on any piece of furniture he finds. And a crate? Hell, no." She gave Rufus a kiss on his head. "My house is your house, got it?" A wet kiss on her face hinted at approval.

It didn't take long for Brad to pack his truck and check out in the office. "Now we can take that walk," he said smiling, sliding off his sneakers at the edge of the sand. "Ready for another 'almost normal' father-daughter activity?"

Carla laughed, her flip flops flying as she kicked them off. "I like the sound of that."

"The almost normal?" Brad teased.

"No...the father – daughter part."

Brad retrieved her flip flops and handed them to her. "Come on. Let's go make some more memories." And then, with a twinkle in his eye, he added, "Race ya!"

She watched him take off toward the water with Rufus bounding along in front, already barking at sandpipers along the shore. *God, this feels so amazing. Nonna, if you're up there, can you fill the house with good energy when we get there? Ya know, when I bring my Dad home?*

With joyful energy, she took off to catch up to a dad with his dog. Her dad.

———

Later that day, she was sitting on her bed reading, with Rufus curled up on the quilt next to her liked he'd always owned the bed. "Just so you know," she told him, "that spot belongs to Paul when he's here, so don't get too comfortable." She chuckled at the quiet thumping of his tail in response.

His ears perked up suddenly, as movement from Carla's old room – now a guest room – signaled Brad's nap had ended. Rufus sat up, staying on the bed, but greeting his owner with vigorous tail swishes across the quilt. Brad leaned against the door jam, looking refreshed.

"I see someone's made himself at home."

"I told him he'll have to relocate when Paul is here – but it's been nice having him curled up next to me."

Brad noticed the quilt on the bed. "Wow...that's a flash from the past. Elena's quilt."

"You remember it?"

"How could I not? With all the stories she told?" He stepped forward and scanned for one spot in the middle of the bed. "See the little stain on that one? You did that."

"Don't I know it. She told me many times of the day I tried her coffee and spit it out."

Brad's laugh warmed her heart. "I would have waited until you were two before giving you some. Glad you changed your mind about liking the stuff." He gestured toward the chair in the corner. "Mind if I sit?"

"By all means." Carla closed her book and placed it on the nightstand beside her, which caught Brad's attention.

"Wow...you still have that."

"The book?" Carla asked, holding up a tattered copy of Ray Bradbury's *Fahrenheit 451*. "It was on a bookshelf down in the basement – I think it was my grandad's."

"Open it up to page 31," Brad said, a grin on his face. "Bet you'll find the page number is circled."

Carla's heart raced, remembering the circle when she'd read the page, and realizing now it's implication. She'd been reading her dad's book. "This was yours?"

He nodded. "We'd come over to visit some Sundays, and your mom would go off shopping with one of her friends when you napped. I ended up leaving a small stack here for when Elena turned on the television."

"Must have been the Pats games if it was a Sunday. Any other day it was game shows. As for this," she continued, holding up the book, "I wasn't sure I'd like it – but man, the parallels to everything going on around us today – almost scary."

"That's my favorite all time book, I'll have you know."

"Sorry it got a little musty in the basement – there's another one by Bradbury down there, along with a few by Ludlum."

"Ah, The Bourne trilogy...read any of those yet?"

"Don't laugh, but those are thicker books – and I didn't really start reading until Nonna started to fade away."

"You should give him a try – they're fast reads once things start moving." Brad's gaze rested on the nightstand, a pensive look on his face. "That nightstand...I don't know if Nonna ever told you, but that's mine, too. I made it for her the last Christmas I was here...and she kept it all these years."

Carla's hand caressed the old wood as tears filled her eyes. "You...made this? So, your energy has been in this house all along, and I never knew. This has always been one of my favorite things in the house – and Nonna could have shared so much about you...but she didn't."

Brad came over and sat on the bed, welcoming Carla into his arms. He held her as she cried, feeling as cheated as she did from the unshared memories. Rufus skootched over to place his head on her leg, his tail wagging slightly.

Carla let the tears flow – cleansing tears...healing tears. Her dad was holding her, and for the first time in her life, that made everything okay.

# CHAPTER TWENTY

Hannah sat on a bench overlooking Salem Harbor. After a day visiting the House of Seven Gables and other witchy haunts, she felt revitalized. *I needed a day alone on the beach today. Now I feel ready to follow my heart – and the hell with what other people think.* She'd sketched a preliminary logo idea for Eastern Point Tarot – the name she would use for her new business.

She didn't hear JJ's approach until he practically leaped over the bench to sit next to her.

"How'd it go?"

"It was a long day just sitting," JJ said. "Neck is killing me."

Hannah stood up behind him, reaching out to massage his shoulders. "Here, let me. How do you think you did?"

JJ moaned as Hannah's fingers massaged the tension away. "Oh, that feels so good..."

"I can feel all the tension; you're really tight." She leaned forward, pressing against him as her hair brushed his face. "And you still haven't answered the question."

She didn't expect him to reach up and pull her arms down close to his chest, turning his head to kiss her. "I couldn't have done any of this without you. You have no idea how much it all means."

Hannah kissed his cheek and hugged him from behind, aware of every place their bodies touched. She rested her head on his shoulder as they gazed out toward the open sea. "I think I have a pretty good idea," she whispered. "It means freedom for you—and you've worked so hard for it."

JJ shifted on the bench, patting the spot beside him. "I want this so bad; it'll let me finally put my mistakes behind me. My community service hours will be done by the end of the month, and if I get this, I'll have a chance to get a real job, doing what I love. And it's all because of you."

He leaned in and kissed her again, this time with more urgency. "I can't wait to finally celebrate freedom with you."

She welcomed his kiss, feeling the desire between them, anticipating what that freedom would bring. No more curfews, and no need to follow unspoken rules by the man who held JJ a prisoner in his own home. They had yet to be together, but they both sensed the promise of that union approaching.

"Me, too," she whispered, "Although I'm not sure your folks are gonna approve of you being with a pagan."

JJ laughed. "Oh, I'll go further than that; I'm gonna tell them I'm in love with a witch."

Hannah froze. "Did you...just say love?"

JJ pulled her close. "Damn right I did. I love you, Hannah. I think I've loved you—"

Her kiss back told him everything he needed to know.

———

On the drive back to Gloucester, Hannah told him about her decision to start her own business, and he talked about finding a job as a builder. GED results would be posted online some time the next day, and they made plans to spend the day together again.

"I want the woman I love to be there when I push that button for results," JJ said.

Hannah's cheeks glowed every time he said the word. She reached over and squeezed his hand. "I wouldn't wanna be anywhere else when the man I love finds out he passed."

Shortly after they passed Hammond Castle, JJ was surprised to find Hannah pulling in to the driveway of one of his mom's friends, Peg Fernandez. She had never married, and lived in the house her parents had built with her nine cats. She also had several young people renting rooms to help pay the bills, including Terri and Nate's son Vinny.

"What are we stopping here for?"

Hannah grinned. "I heard from Vinny that Sofia is moving out next week – she got a big promotion and decided it was time to get an apartment on her own. I didn't know if you might be interested in—"

"A room of my own? Oh, hell, yeah!"

JJ almost jumped out of the car, wrapping his arms around Hannah and pulling her close. "A place for us to finally be together when we want..."

"Yeah, I suspect Peg is pretty open minded about overnight guests. As long as you like cats."

Two orange tabbies were curled up on the front porch chairs, hardly acknowledging their presence as they passed by to ring the bell. Peg answered the door, ushering them in with a smile. "Come on in. Hannah had called earlier and said you might stop by. Make yourself at home, and we can chat. You hungry? Vinny made a huge pan of mac & cheese earlier."

"Sounds great," JJ said. "I'm famished. Now I know why she didn't wanna eat in Salem...my sneaky witch."

They followed Peg through a living room adorned with cat paraphernalia everywhere, passing three black cats perched on the furniture. "That's Rosie, Midnight, and Bagheera," Peg explained, "And you saw Franklin and Garfield out on the porch, I'm sure. There's four more wandering around – if you can handle cats, you're more than welcome to check out the room upstairs across from Vinny, or Sofia's room on this floor. She's over at her new place painting, and most of her room is packed up. Gonna miss having my tech guru down the hall. Second door on the right – go take a look around while I get plates out."

Hannah led JJ down the hall, stopping to greet a small black cat with a tail up to greet them. "This must be Little Black Cat," Hannah said, listening to a giant purr coming out of the small body. "Vinny said she was a total lovebug."

"Original name; I like it."

The door to Sofia's room was open, and JJ smiled when he stepped inside. "Nice light – and I like the view out toward the woods." He gestured toward the twin bed Sofia had up against the wall. "Might need a new bed, though..." He wrapped his arms around Hannah. "In case I have company."

Hannah felt the electricity between them, and gave him a playful push away. "All in good time, you. I think you're supposed to be looking at the room to see if it'll work for you. Plenty of closet space, and a nice desk – although this could be Sofia's."

"Trust me," JJ said, "All I need is a place where I can live my own life on my terms. I take it Peg is pretty cool with rules?"

"I get that feeling from Vinny, but that's why we're here. Come on, I'll give you a tour of the rest of the place. I've been here a few times with my mom." She led JJ across the hall to Peg's office, with more cat decorations, as well as posters of Gloria Steinem and Ruth Bader Ginsberg on the one wall without bookshelves. A big desk was wedged in the corner, covered with papers, books, and Peg's computer. A police scanner sat atop a filing cabinet behind the door.

"Positive and productive vibes in this room," JJ said. "I get a really good feeling about Peg from all this."

"Yeah, I think you'll like her a lot. She's probably my favorite of Mom's friends – independent and quirky, like me."

"Come on, let's go check out the room upstairs."

As soon as they looked in, JJ nodded. "Oh, man, this is it. What a room." A black cat was curled up on a full sized brass bed tucked between the slanting roof. She jumped down and scooted under the bed as they entered. "Jeez, they are everywhere, aren't they?"

Hannah got down on her knees and coaxed the feline out. "This one is Mitzi; Vinny said she camped out upstairs; she's shy, but a real sweetie." The cat sniffed Hannah's hand and welcomed the scratch behind the ears.

JJ reached down to run his hands over Mitzi's back, and her purr got louder.

"I think she approves," Hannah whispered.

"This room has character," JJ said. "I love it." Two small closets were built into the eaves on either side of the bed, and small dormers at the front and back of the room made space for a bureau and a desk.

He sat down on the bed and laughed at the squeak. "New mattress, though. That's a definite."

"You're incorrigible," Hannah teased. "But that does look pretty old. Come on, let's go down and talk logistics." Mitzi jumped back up on the bed, and rubbed up against JJ's arm.

"I think she's made it clear that you're now one of her humans – and you're meant to be here."

JJ scratched under Mitzi's chin. "You've got yourself a servant, my lady. But not until we eat – I smell mac and cheese, and I'm hungry."

# CHAPTER TWENTY-ONE

Carla caught Joey staring at her as she wrapped utensils for the next day. "What's with you, boss?"

"Nothin'. Just noticing how different you are lately."

Carla rolled her eyes. "I don't what you're talking about."

Joey wiped down the far end of the bar. "The hell you don't. Between dating Paul and having your dad here, you haven't stopped smiling all week. Happiness looks good on you, Squirt."

Carla slid the finished tray under the bar. "Feels good, too – not gonna lie. Sometimes I have to pinch myself to make sure it's real. Or look over my shoulder to see what's coming to wreck it all."

"So, where *is* your dad tonight? I thought you said he was coming in to see how you run the place."

"No, *you* say that, boss, not me." Carla waved to two regular customers as they left, and passed Joey to clear their booth out. "He's actually been hanging out with Paul today. Said he might look up a couple of old timers he worked with years ago to see if they're still down on the docks."

"I'm sure he'll find a few still around," Joey replied. "By the way, you free to come in a little early tomorrow?"

Carla turned around, leaning on the booth table. "How early? You know I'm not a morning person."

"I have a noon appointment; was hoping you could come in beforehand. I'll bring you lunch when I come back – name the place."

Carla laughed. "You know damn well how to win me over. Bring me a pepperoni pizza from Bruno's and you've got yourself a deal."

Before Joey replied, Paul and Brad's laughter announced their arrival.

"Welcome to Carla's other home," Paul teased, flashing her a smile that weakened her knees.

Brad smiled as well, but turned his attention to Joey. "You old codger – you're still around?"

Joey opened his arms wide. "Welcome back...you're lookin' good."

"Wait, you two *know* each other?" Carla whacked her boss on the arm. "And you didn't *tell* me?"

"Relax, Squirt. It was a long time ago, and I stay outta peoples' business – even yours."

"But that's bullshit! You could have told me all kinds of stuff about my dad, and you *didn't?*"

"Hey, watch the mouth – there are still people in the back."

Carla turned her back on him. Dirty dishes rattled as she almost threw them into the bin she was using.

Brad and Paul held back as Joey place his arm around Carla's shoulder. She flinched, but didn't push him away.

"Listen – it wasn't my place. What if I *had* told you? Would you have been happier, or maybe more pissed off than you already were? I wanted to give you a safe space here, that's all. Truce?"

"Maybe..."

Paul approached and wrapped his arms around her from behind. "You were lucky Joey kept you around all these years; he's gotten you through some tough times."

Brad agreed. "When you told me you worked here, I knew you were in good hands. I'm grateful someone watched over you."

"Glad to do it," Joey said. "Besides, I like having her around. I'd have to *work* if she wasn't here."

Carla picked up the bin of dishes, taking advantage of the lighter mood. "You *still* coulda told me," she chided, but she grinned as she placed the bin on the bar. "And *you,*" she said turning to Brad, "Sounds like you were a regular."

"I spent a fair amount of time in here." He patted a stool beside him. "Maybe on this very stool."

Carla hopped up onto the stool next to him with Paul on her other side. "It never occurred to me that you'd be here – but I guess it makes sense. I know this place was busier back then."

"Place was hoppin'," Joey said, his eyes twinkling as he walked back behind the bar. "We got the high school kids wolfing down burgers and fries in the afternoon, the guys coming off the docks before heading home, and the regulars at night, playing pool and darts."

"Guilty as charged," Brad replied.

Joey placed a beer in front of each of them, but stopped when he got to Brad, who held up a worn sobriety chip with the number twenty in roman numerals.

The old man moved the beer aside. "Good for you. What can I get ya instead?"

"Club soda with lemon and any kind of juice – and thanks."

"I'm proud of you," Carla whispered, as Brad placed the chip on the bar in front of him. She noted the small smile as Joey returned with his drink.

"I think you've got a lot to stay sober for," Joey said.

Brad nodded, meeting his daughter's gaze. "Don't I know it." Lifting his glass, he continued. "To good times."

As Carla sipped the cold brew, laughter erupted from the pool room as two middle aged-women came into view. The blonde woman stumbled a bit, holding her beer mug upside down as the other kept her steady. "S'all gone..." the drunk one slurred. "That's sad..."

Her friend was far less intoxicated. "No, that means it's time for me to take you home." Her gaze met Carla's. "Boyfriend broke up with her," she explained. "Figured this was a safe place to bring her where she'd be least likely to go home with someone."

"But this one's CUUTE…" The blonde stopped next to Brad's stool. "Hel-LO, han'some…"

Brad leaned back, his palms up in front of him. "Sorry…not interested."

"Come on, Stacey, let's get you out of here so these nice people can go home." She flashed Brad a smile as they headed past. "She won't even remember in the morning."

Paul grinned as the women walked out. "You could have had an easy date tonight, pal."

"Definitely not in the market right now. The only woman I'm interested in getting to know better is sitting beside me." His voice dropped to a whisper only his daughter could hear. "I mean that, you know."

"I'm trying to believe it…but keep telling me, okay?"

"You betcha," he replied, swallowing the last of his drink.

# CHAPTER TWENTY-TWO

Carla reported to work early the next day; Rod & Bernie, two retired dock workers, were eating lunch on their regular stools. Even without looking, she knew they were eating hot pastrami sandwiches and fries. *I swear they've eaten the same lunch every day for the past ten years at least.*

"What brings you in so early?" Rod asked.

"Boss wanted me here."

"Better not be firing ya," Bernie mumbled, his mouth full of fries.

"Not a chance in hell of that." Joey laughed as he appeared from the kitchen. "Who the hell would run the place – one of you?"

Carla laughed along with the guys. "I probably *could* have left the two of you in charge."

Joey grabbed his coat from the rack by the bar. "I won't be long. Thanks for coming in."

"Everything okay?"

"I'd tell ya if it wasn't, wouldn't I? By the way, I asked Gino to come in to close tonight, so you can take off at six. Thought you might like some extra time with your dad. Can't be easy for him having to visit a bar every time he wants to hang out with his daughter."

"Actually," Carla replied, "He's staying at the house for the rest of his visit, so it'll be nice to make him dinner tonight – thanks, boss."

After Joey left, Carla refilled drinks for the regulars and took two phone orders for lunch, which she had ready by the door when folks came in to pick them up. She straightened up some menus under the bar, and spotted a folder beneath the pile.

*He's always misplacing stuff from his desk. He'll be looking for this tomorrow and wondering where it is.* As she pulled it out to return it to the kitchen, a business card slid out of the folder onto the floor. *Harborside Development Corporation? Why the hell does he have something from them?* Unable to curb her curiosity, she opened the folder and recognized their brochure. They had purchased several older downtown businesses already, and had started to tear them down to build "a revitalized waterfront community around the harbor." *The hell they are. They're taking away all the mom & pop shops to put up fancy condos and coffee shops the locals can't afford. Gonna put the entire fishing community out of business.*

Some handwritten notes were in the side pocket, but they weren't Joey's handwriting. *These look like preliminary figures for an offer. Joey, what the hell are you doing?*

She closed it and left it in plain sight, looking at the clock about thirty times while filling the salt shakers for each booth. Joey returned shortly after 1:00; he kept his head down as he came around the bar, ignoring the greetings from his two loyal lunch customers. Carla's temper simmered as he hung up his coat and waved slightly. "Thanks for covering, Squirt. Pizza's coming in the next few minutes."

He walked back into the kitchen without another word. *He thinks he's gonna slither in there and hide? Hell, no!* Grabbing the folder from the counter, she followed her boss and slapped it on butcher block where he was putting on his apron.

"Is *this* what your damn meeting was about? Gonna sell this place without even telling me? Am I really worth that little to you?" Her chest heaved as Joey slumped back against the counter and folded his hands against his chest.

"I'd like to tell you not to jump to conclusions, but I guess I'm too late for that."

"You're not answering the question."

"Before you fly off the handle, *no,* I'm not selling, okay? Jeez, you always go to the worst case scenario. Where did you find that, anyway?"

"It was under the bar; I wasn't snooping. And yeah, sometimes I over react – but what the hell, boss? What was I supposed to think? They've already knocked down three other places, and they gotta be salivating over this stretch by the pier."

Joey smirked. "Yeah, I think you have them all figured out. They sure were smooth talkers."

Carla pointed to handwritten note. "Is this a ballpark offer? They'd give you that much for this place?"

Joey closed the folder. "Don't matter. I'm not selling." He picked up a knife and a few onions on the counter. "Now let me get back to work, will ya? Go wait for your pizza – and your job is secure for as long as you want it."

"What the hell does *that* mean? And what was your appointment for?"

Joey sliced into the onion, not looking at Carla as he answered. "If you must know, my nosy little Squirt, I was at my lawyer's up the street. Made a change in my will."

"Your will?" Carla's tone softened. "Are you okay, boss? Not sick or anything?"

The old man grinned and met her gaze. "I'm probably healthier than you are. I made a change so the developers will stop bugging me for good."

"What do you mean?"

"I'm leaving it to you after I'm gone – so *you* can deal with Harborside from now on."

"What? You're giving the Keel to *me?*" Carla took a step toward Joey, who put down his knife and turned toward her.

"Who else?" Joey replied. "My brother and niece left this town decades ago, and they'd sell out to Harborside before my body was cold. But you might bring it back to life."

Carla stood frozen as Joey's words took hold. "You're serious, aren't you?"

He gently placed his hands on her shoulders and met her gaze. "I'm hoping to be around for a long time yet, but I'd like you to start taking charge...I think 'Carla's Place' has a nice ring to it, don't you?"

"I...don't know what to say..."

The bell rang out front, and Joey gave her a nudge. "That's probably Bruno's – go eat your pizza and we can talk more later."

————

When Carla arrived home later on, the smells of garlic and onion greeted her along with welcoming barks from Rufus. Brad was at the stove, with a pot of boiling water and a big pan with spaghetti sauce.

"I thought I was cooking for *you*," she teased. She hung her coat behind the door and knelt down for wet kisses from Rufus. "Have you been a good boy?"

"Hope you don't mind the change," Brad replied. "I haven't cooked since we left Nova Scotia, and I missed it. Figured I could handle spaghetti. I made extra for Paul."

He placed the pasta in the pot as Carla grabbed the wooden spoon beside the sauce, giving it a taste. "Hmm...this is awesome. And I texted Paul to tell him I was getting out early, but I wasn't sure if you'd want him around for dinner."

Brad laughed. "He must be confused then; I called to invite him. I get the feeling he's used to being around here lately. He...talks about you a *lot*, by the way. Pretty obvious that he really cares about you."

"Sometimes I wonder how I got so lucky," Carla said, taking three plates out of the cabinet for the table. "First Paul shows up, and now you're here – and then Joey's bombshell today—"

"What bombshell?"

The doorbell rang before Carla could answer. "That'll be Paul – and I'll explain over spaghetti."

Brad brought up the question again once dinner was well under way. "So...you gonna tell us the big news, or do we have to guess?"

"What news?" Paul mumbled with a mouth full of food.

Carla put her fork down and took a deep breath. "Okay...so here's the thing...Joey got an offer for the bar from the development company that's been building the new condos by the waterfront."

"He's selling the Keel?" Brad asked. "After all these years?"

"Nope--turned them down. He doesn't want the place torn down like some of the other old businesses."

"I agree with him on that," Paul said. "On the other hand, he's not getting any younger."

"Yeah, well, that's why I got called in early – Joey had an appointment with his lawyer. He's leaving the Keel to me, and wants me to start running it now."

"Are you kidding?" Brad almost knocked his chair over from jumping up to give her a hug. "That's awesome news!"

Paul was right behind him. "Nobody else loves the place like you do – and Joey knows it."

"I just hope he's not screwing over his retirement," Carla said as they resumed eating. "I hope I can keep the place going for a while. Business sure ain't what it used to be."

"What the place needs..." Brad swallowed his mouthful before continuing. "...is some renovation. Nothing big – new appliances in the kitchen, some fresh paint, and maybe a new floor? Those few things alone might make a huge difference."

"Needs more than that," Paul added. "That old sign out front needs replacing. Paint is peeling so bad, only the locals know what it's called. Whole outside needs a little sprucing up to attract the tourists."

Carla put her hands up. "Whoa! Your ideas might be good, but Joey's still in charge, and I doubt he has that kind of money. Not like we get tourists coming in anyway."

Paul didn't back down. "But you *could*. It's a great location to grab them coming back from whale watching or visiting the waterfront. I think you could bring this place back to life!"

"Again...there's a little question of money."

"I think he's on to something," Brad replied. "Joey's still the boss, but if he wants you to start really running it, then he might be on board. You could apply for a loan."

"Me? You think my credit's gonna land me a business loan?"

"You've been working there forever," Paul offered, "And now you're a home owner. You might be surprised."

"He's right," Brad continued. "I could go with you to the bank to talk to someone, if you'd like."

"You'd...do that for me?"

"It would mean a lot if you'd let me. I wish I could hand over the money you need, but I'm not rich." Brad paused before continuing. "Maybe you should consider asking your—"

"Don't even *think* about mentioning her name! She's never given anything more than a couple of bills tucked inside birthday or Christmas cards, and I wouldn't ask her for a penny."

"Why not?" Paul chimed in. "The worst she can do is say 'no,' but she might surprise you."

"How the hell can you even suggest it?" Carla fumed.

"Because she owes you, that's why. She owes you way more than the cost of renovations, and she's got a ton of it in the bank."

Carla stood up so fast her chair almost fell over. "I don't want a stinking *dime* of her money!" She grabbed her dish and almost dropped it in the sink. "I can't believe you of all people don't know that, after everything we've talked about!"

"Honey, he's just trying to help," Brad said. "It's something to file away, just in case a loan doesn't work out."

Carla spun around, glaring at both of them. "What the hell is wrong with you two? I thought we'd have a nice relaxing night, and instead you're ruining it!"

"How are we ruining anything?" Paul asked, placing his dish on the counter. "I just hate to see how that woman keeps you feeling like you're not enough. She's got more money than she'll ever spend, and it would pay for your future as a business owner to have some."

Carla whacked him on the arm. "You know damn well there's no way in hell I'd ask! I've had enough rejection from her to last a lifetime!"

"How about we table this discussion for—"

"Look, Dad...I don't need parental advice right now, okay? And I'm

not in the mood for hanging out tonight. You two can do something."
She started down the hall toward her room.

"It's not her rejection that's getting in the way!" Paul called after
her. "It's because you're too damn proud to admit that you could use
her help, and too damn scared to ask because she might actually say
yes!"

Carla spun around to challenge him, only to see him slam the door
on his way out.

"Honey, I'm so sorry—"

"Don't even!" Carla choked out. She ran past Rufus and closed the
door on both of them, flopping onto her bed as tears spilled over. *I
knew it. I knew it was too good to last. Now he's gone, and my Dad will leave,
too. And I'll be alone again. Just like always.*

# CHAPTER TWENTY-THREE

Carla woke up after a restless night to a quiet house. Her first thought was that Brad and Rufus had left like Paul had, but there was a bag from the Brine & Brew with coffee and a cinnamon roll waiting on the kitchen table. *Thought you could use a treat this morning; had to run a few errands, but we'll be back in a bit. Dad.*

She took a sip of the coffee, running her fingers over the note. *Dad. I never thought I'd find notes on my kitchen table signed 'Dad.'* She took a plate out of the cabinet, noting the clean dishes in the drying rack. *He must have done those last night after my tantrum. I'm surprised he didn't leave, too.*

Images of the night before looped around her brain as she nibbled her pastry. The sound of Paul slamming the door echoed in her ears. She grabbed her phone to see if there were any messages, and sighed to find none. *Paul. Did I lose him last night? Because of my stupid mother? Please, Nonna – don't let him be gone.* She began typing an apology text, but erased the words. *Why am I apologizing? He's the one who stormed out...*

"Who am I kidding? I'm the one who screamed at him – no wonder he had enough." Speaking the words brought a whole new wave of sorrow, and this time she texted a quick "I'm sorry" before finishing her breakfast.

After showering and getting dressed, she checked her phone and sighed. Still nothing. *At least my dad didn't leave – and I owe him a huge apology when he gets back.* She returned to the kitchen, tucking his handwritten note into her pocket for safekeeping, and put all the clean dishes away. She was just finishing up when the front doorbell chimed.

She rushed to the door, assuming it was him and Rufus returning. "Did you forget the key I gave—"

Her words died on her tongue as the open door revealed not Brad, but Paul. For a moment, the silence between them hung in the air.

"You...came back."

"I never should have left like that...I am so—"

"Just shut up and kiss—"

Paul's lips were on hers before she could finish, and she clung to him as the kiss deepened. No words were needed as they made their way down the hallway to Carla's room. They made love with urgency, knowing words would follow, wanting only to recapture the bond between them.

Afterwards, Paul held her gently as emotions flooded through her. *So, this is what it feels like to make up after a fight. Like I never want to let him go.* She nuzzled in closer, tracing her fingers on his chest as her eyes met his. "That was amazing," she whispered.

Paul covered her hand with his and smiled. "*You're* amazing. And to think I was afraid you wouldn't even talk to me when I got here."

"Huh? Why would you think that? Didn't you get my text?"

"You texted me?" Paul reached back behind him and found his phone on the back corner of the nightstand. "I would have called first, but kind of left my phone here when I stormed out."

He read the message waiting for him and kissed Carla on the forehead. "I'm sorry, too, Squirt. I don't know what I was thinking. All I knew this morning was that I had to come back and apologize. I hardly slept last night thinking of how hurt you must have felt."

"I tossed and turned, too. I was thinking you had really left."

"Hold on a sec," Paul said, leaning over the side of the bed to find the coat that had been discarded in a heap with other clothes. He fumbled in the pocket to retrieve a small bag. "I brought you something – thought it might mean more than flowers."

Carla supported herself on one elbow as she opened the small bag to pull out a stuffed Piping Plover – the birds she and Paul had talked about on their first date.

"Remember how you told me they mate for life? I wanted you to know that I wanna be around for as long as you'll have me – hopefully forever." He met Carla's gaze. "I've fallen in love with you, in case you didn't know."

Her eyes filled with tears as she leaned down to kiss him. "I love you, too – more than I ever thought I could." She snuggled in close and welcomed his embrace. "I didn't know if I'd ever feel this way about anyone...but you came along and showed me what love was."

Paul caressed her cheek with his thumb. "You've grown so much since we've been together. You dragged those skeletons from your past out and made room for me to come in, and I wouldn't trade these months for anything."

"Me, neither," Carla whispered. "You...taught me how to trust again."

Paul met her gaze. "That's why last night was so hard; I felt like I'd let you down when I left, and I don't want you to ever feel abandoned because of me."

"It's okay...you came back, and you're here now. That's all that matters."

"I promise you I'm not going anywhere. I want to be here – but you have one more skeleton to deal with, and until you do, you're not gonna be free to move forward."

Carla's eyes filled with tears, and she shook her head. "I...can't. It hurts too much..." His arms pulled her close, and in the refuge of his embrace, she finally let go. "All I ever wanted...was for her to love me..." Her sobs wracked her body in between phrases. "Why...couldn't she do that...why did she just...throw me away?"

Paul stroked her hair as she cried. "Shh..." he whispered. "You're gonna be okay. Just let it all out. Let it all go..."

Carla woke up hours later, still wrapped in his arms, still holding the gift he had brought her. *They mate for life – and so will we.* The quilt was damp from her tears—the quilt that had represented warmth and security all her life, and now she understood why it had meant so much to her grandmother.

*It symbolized the love you had for Nonno, and the life you pieced together in this house. My house now – one I hope to share with Paul someday.* She snuggled in closer, listening to his slow, deep breathing, feeling his chest rise beneath her with his heart beat steady in her ear. And she felt peace.

# CHAPTER TWENTY-FOUR

The meeting at the bank did not go well. Taylor Grayson, the loan officer, took off her glasses and placed them on the desk. "I'll put the application through," she said, "But I wouldn't have high expectations. Your credit's been up and down over the years, and a business loan at this time is not likely to be approved. I'm sorry."

"Even if I were to cosign?" Brad asked.

Taylor closed the folder on her desk. "I know you're her father, and I'm glad you've reunited, but your absence doesn't make you the most credible resource right now." She looked at Carla. "Perhaps a friend or another family—"

"Thank you for your time." Carla swallowed the lump in her throat and stood up with resolve. "Dad, I guess we're done here." She shook the hand that Taylor extended across the desk before hurrying out the door.

Brad caught up with her out on the sidewalk. "Hey...slow down. It'll work out."

Carla blinked back tears as she faced him. "Yeah, it's gonna be great. I'll run the bar into the ground while you head on back to Canada."

"Honey, I told you it might a long shot today – but at least we tried.

In the meantime," he said, pulling an envelope out of his pocket, "I want you to have this. I wish it was more, but it's all I can give you right now. You can at least slap some paint on the walls."

Carla looked at the envelope. "I can't take money from you..."

"Why the hell not? I'm your father, and I want to help."

"You've only been back in my life for two weeks, Dad...you're not obliged to help me out. Especially since you're hopping back in your truck and heading home."

"Are you kidding?" Brad grabbed Carla's arm. "I'm not leaving till we talk this out."

Carla looked at the people bustling by and tried to hold her tears back. "Not *here*."

Brad looked around and led her to a bench farther back from the road. "No one will notice us back here. Come sit. You make it sound like I'm trying to pay off a guilty conscience before taking off again." He shook his head. "I thought the last two weeks meant more than that to you."

"Damn it, it's nothing like that!" Carla didn't even try to hold back the tears. "These two weeks have meant *everything* to me! Do you have any idea how hard it is to watch you get into your truck and leave?"

Brad scooted over closer and pulled Carla into a hug. "Trust me," he whispered into her hair. "I know exactly how hard it is." He squeezed her hard, then pulled back and wiped her wet cheeks with his thumbs. "But honey, not all goodbyes are forever."

Carla looked down at his sweater. "I'm just not that good with goodbyes..."

He gently lifted her chin to meet her gaze. "I can't wait until I'm back for Christmas. It's gonna be the best one ever, I promise."

"It's kind of a low bar to beat," Carla chuckled. "And you'll have to be patient with me; I haven't had a lot of practice with trusting people to come back."

"I promise you'll get lot of practice for a while. I hope to be down here as much as I can in between jobs – if you'll have me."

"Only if you bring Rufus every time."

Brad laughed out loud, and Carla's shoulders relaxed. He took her hand, placed the envelope in it, and folded her fingers over it. "As for the guilt, I can't lie and say I don't feel guilty about not being there for you. It consumed me for years until I got sober, and maybe it's part of why I've kept my sobriety. I have a lot of things to make up to you, but it's more about love and gratitude than guilt right now, because I get a second chance with my daughter." He released her hand, and sat up straight. "So, you get yourself some paint, and think of me with every brush stroke, okay?"

"Okay." Carla took the envelope and shoved it in her pocket. "Promise you'll text along the way?"

"We'll be stopping in Bangor for something to eat and a stretch, so expect an update mid to late afternoon."

"How much farther after that?"

"It's another few hours to St. John in New Brunswick; we'll crash there tonight and hop on the ferry tomorrow morning over to Digby – cuts the driving time way down."

"Must be a beautiful ride."

"Maybe next summer we can do it together? I can show you Peggy's Cove."

"I'd love that."

Brad chuckled. "It'll make Gloucester look like a thriving metropolis." He glanced at his watch. "And if I'm gonna get there by tomorrow, I gotta get on the road soon."

Carla nodded, sensing it was time for the inevitable parting. "Can you do me a favor?"

"Name it."

"Can you sit here for a few minutes until I'm gone? I don't think I can watch you drive away – and I have to get to work anyway."

"I can do that," Brad choked out. "for you." He stood up and gave her a long hug. "I'm gonna miss you, kiddo – but I'll be back soon. I promise."

Carla nodded, her face buried in his sweater, breathing in his musky scent, tinged with salt from all their walks outside. *He'll come back. I have to believe him. I need to believe him.* With one final squeeze, she glanced up at his face and smiled. "Safe travels..." was all she could manage to say before bolting up the street toward her car.

He watched her go, wondering how he could feel so much love and so much sadness at the same time. As promised, he sat back down to wait until she was safely on her way to the sanctuary of the bar and Joey's protective care. *She'll be okay until I get back. She has Joey, and Paul. And I've got Rufus.*

He watched two sparrows fighting over a piece of someone's discarded sandwich crust until enough time had passed. He sighed deeply, ready to head back to his truck where Rufus was no doubt sound asleep. *Time to head north.* The sound of laughter jolted him as he checked the time on his phone. He'd recognize that laugh anywhere, even after all these years.

Betty Sue. She stood only a car length away, her hair catching the sunlight as she chatted with another woman. He prayed she wouldn't glance toward him. *I'm not ready for that meeting yet. But God, she still looks amazing.* He watched as she embraced the other woman and turned to walk past him. He kept his head down, staring at his phone. *Please don't see me. Please.* While part of him wanted to jump up and chase after her, pulling her back into his arms, he instead listened to her footsteps as she moved farther up the street and out of sight, and then waited another couple of minutes before daring to get up. He was grateful that Carla had insisted on this out of the way bench; otherwise, they would have come face to face.

*That was close. God, I know that meeting is gonna come someday, but I don't think I can handle it yet. Right now, I just wanna get to my truck and escape. Then I can figure out how I'm gonna be here with the daughter I want back in my life, and whether to avoid the woman who almost destroyed me — the one I'm still in love with after all this time.*

# CHAPTER TWENTY-FIVE

Carla arrived at the Even Keel to find Rod and Bernie on their stools, and she could hear Joey singing as he cooked.

"Early again?" Rod asked. "What's the occasion today?"

"Yeah, our meal's not even out yet," Bernie added. "But you could pour our coffee."

Carla passed by them in silence, pouring them each a cup before taking off her coat.

"Who you talking to at this—" Joey stuck his head out of the kitchen and grinned when he saw Carla. "Well, well, I like this new schedule. Maybe *you* can make their lunch tomorrow."

"Don't bet on it," Carla replied. She walked down to the other end of the bar and grabbed a container of salt to refill the shakers.

"Well, someone's kind of grumpy," Rod said.

"Let her be," Joey whispered. "I'll be right back with your food." He returned within minutes, and Carla was halfway through her task by the time he approached. "You doing okay, Squirt?"

"It was hard saying goodbye."

"That explains you being here; didn't wanna go home to an empty house, huh?"

"I couldn't handle it right now. But don't worry, I'll stay through closing, and then go home to crash."

Joey leaned in close. "He *will* come back; I hope you believe that."

"I'm trying, boss. It's not easy with my track record."

"You'll feel more confident when he calls. And since you're here, let's grab some coffee and you can tell me about your meeting at the bank."

"Yeah, well that won't take long," Carla scowled. "I won't hold my breath on the loan; the guy basically said no." She slid the bin with full shakers to the other side of the bar. "Not like I was expecting anything."

Joey blocked her from passing by. "The salt can wait. Come in the kitchen and talk to me while I fill a few phone orders."

By the time he was done cooking and Carla packed the food for pickup, her spirits were better. Joey knew how to make her laugh and look for the positive, and as the afternoon wore on, she'd come up with another option for securing the renovations loan. *If anyone's gonna agree to cosign for me, it's her. I hope she's open to the idea.*

In between helping customers, she took inventory of needed items as she often did for Joey. She couldn't count how many times she'd glanced at the clock during the day, but her phone finally rang, and her heart almost skipped a beat when she saw the number. "Hey, you must in Maine by now." *He called. Like he said he would.* Her shoulders relaxed, letting go of the tension she'd been carrying around all day.

"Yep. Rufus and I stretched our legs, and grabbed a burger and fries for the road. Miss you already, kiddo."

"I miss you, too...Dad." It was still awkward using that name, but each time Carla couldn't help but smile. "Promise you'll call me when you get to St. John?"

Brad laughed. "Trying to get rid of me, huh?"

"No, nothing like that! I'm just happy that you—"

"Hey, I'm kidding." Brad's voice was reassuring. "Can I tell you how much the past couple of weeks meant to me?"

Carla blinked back the tears. "Me, too. I'll have to thank Hannah for being on social media and finding you."

"I have a better idea. I think she should help you set up your *own* page, and you can be my friend and leave sarcastic comments on all my photos."

"Don't think I won't," Carla chuckled.

"You doing all right? I know you were pretty bummed after the bank meeting."

"I'm okay, and I'm gonna ask someone else to cosign for me."

"Carla, I need to tell you something before hitting the road—"

The bell signaled new customers arriving. "Dad, I gotta go, unless you can tell me quick."

"Never mind," Brad sighed. "It'll keep. I'll call you tonight when I get to the ferry. I promise."

"Safe travels, okay? Talk to you later."

"You bet. Rufus sends a big wet kiss – and I'll throw in a hug."

"Bye, Dad." *He called. And he'll call again later. And damn it, I have a dad.* She tucked her phone into her apron, picked up menus, and greeted the couple in the back booth with a smile. "Can I bring you coffee or water?" She recognized both of them; they came in every few weeks, and almost always ordered the same thing. "Mushroom burger with Swiss, with ranch dressing for your fries, and fish and chips with extra tartar sauce. How'd I do?"

They slid the menus back toward her without having opened them. "How do you keep track of every person who comes in here?" the woman asked.

Carla grinned. "Lots of practice. And a decent memory helps. I'll get this right in for you." *Not like there's a ton of customers to remember. But maybe I CAN run this place with a little help, and start bringing in more people.* She delivered the order to Joey, and the bell rang again as she came out of the kitchen.

This one made her heart sing, as Paul perched on what had become his regular stool. "Well, you're in a better mood than I thought you might be. Maybe you don't need cheering up." He leaned over the bar to kiss her. "I take it you heard from Brad."

She nodded. "A few minutes ago. God, I'm gonna miss him."

"He'll be back soon enough." Paul reached out for her hand. "I'll keep you company whenever you're lonely."

"Hmm...I could get used to having you around."

"Good to know, 'cause I really love this little harbor town – but only if you're here."

Carla smiled. "Ya know, after so many years of wanting to escape, Gloucester is feeling more like *home* all the time."

———

Carla headed across the street early the next morning to have coffee with Jean. As expected, the latter agreed to cosign the loan, but wanted further discussion.

"I know I'll always be your second mom," Jean said, "But now that Nonna has passed, it's time to figure out what's going on with your real one."

Carla leaned back and sighed. "Paul said the same thing. Told me I'd never move on if I didn't deal with her."

"Sounds like a wise man you've found."

"I don't ever wanna lose him. He's brought...*peace* to my life. But he hasn't been here to see all the crap between Mom and me. He tells me to just let it all go – but how the hell do I *do* that?"

"Honey, you even asking that question shows so much growth. I don't know if it's Paul, or Brad – probably both – but they've softened you a bit."

"Yeah, right," Carla scowled. "You should have heard me screaming about her the other night. Paul actually walked out on me."

"Everything okay?"

Carla nodded. "He came back the next day, and I think we've gotten even closer after talking through it."

"Well, that's what reconciliation is all about. Working through the hurt's the only way to get to other side."

"You're talking about my mother now, aren't you?"

Jean reached over to grasp Carla's hand. "You know how much I love both of you. And I've seen you both growing in the past couple of months. I think deep down inside, you both want some healing – maybe even a chance for some of a relationship."

Carla pulled her hand back. "Yeah, right. Like that's ever gonna happen."

"You would have said the same thing about your dad not too long ago," Jean continued.

"Don't compare the two of them, okay?"

Jean pressed on. "Honey, I know there's so much more anger to work through with your mom, and it doesn't have to happen overnight – but I think you two are at a place now where you could at least be open to the possibilities."

"What possibility? To let her hurt me again? There's nothing left between us."

"I don't believe either of you on that. I think buried under all your anger and all her guilt is a desire to heal. Maybe you'll never be close, but wouldn't it bring a whole lot of peace to work through the crap once and for all?"

"Why bother?" Carla's voice cracked.

"Because Paul and Brad have shown you what love can do – if you're brave enough."

"I don't know if I am with her," Carla said, blinking back tears. "And I wouldn't have a clue where to even begin."

Jean passed over a box of tissues from the side table. "I actually might have an idea for that." She met Carla's gaze and continued. "It's about the money for the loan."

"Hell, no! I'm not taking her money!"

"I didn't say that," Jean countered calmly. "What I'm suggesting is that you ask her to cosign the loan instead—"

"What good would it do? She'd either try to give me the money, or judge me for asking."

"Or maybe, *if* you can talk to her without flying off the handle, she'd recognize it as a bridge being offered between the two of you. A way to acknowledge you're both at least open to a connection that might help build some trust down the road."

"I don't know if I'm ready for that. Maybe if I wait—"

"Wait for what?" Jean asked. "The only way things are going to change is if you do something different than you've been doing all these years. Look at Paul and Brad – did you sit and *think* about either of them, or did you take a chance and put yourself out there?"

Carla wondered if Jean could hear her heart racing. "Would you... come with me? I don't think I could face her on my own."

"There's nothing in this whole world I'd rather do." She stood up and gave Carla a hug. "Come on, let's go talk to your mom."

# CHAPTER TWENTY-SIX

Jean called Betty Sue to let them know the two of them were going to stop by. Carla followed in her own car, and voiced her concerns again after pulling in next to Jean. "If she tries to give me the money, will you still cosign the loan if I refuse her?"

"You know I will – but what makes you think she won't agree?"

"It's not that she won't do it; I just hate the idea of her bragging about it to her friends – how 'generous' she is. I don't want to owe her anything in this."

"I think you might be projecting a bit there," Jean replied, leaning against Carla's car. "Your mom has had some epiphanies about her money lately, and I think she's trying to use it in some really healthy ways right now."

"What do you mean?"

"She's finally recognized the value of giving back. She's paid for Terri to continue her physical therapy, and I know she covered some of Nate's doctor bills as well – all done anonymously."

Carla stared at her mom's front door. "I guess that's something."

"And you don't know about her newest work with the Chamber of Commerce."

"Huh?"

"I wanted her to tell you about it, but your mom's joined the board of a foundation that's giving grants to young women starting their own businesses in town – and has donated a lot of the funding for the project."

Carla whacked the top of her car. "She *what?* So, she didn't give me a penny, but now she's helping a bunch of others with their stuff? Like, what the hell? And why am I even here?"

"Honey, she's trying. She knows she screwed up with you, and I think she'd love to hand you a bunch of cash if she thought it would make a difference. But I agree with you on needing to do this on your own. Let her cosign the loan, but prove to yourself that you can run the business without her help."

Carla stared down at the pavement, shivering a bit, despite the unseasonable warmth in the air. "Why couldn't she have done things differently? I hate being here and not having a clue about what to even say to her."

Jean reached out and squeezed her hand. "You'll be fine – I promise."

Betty Sue let them in, gesturing toward the open door onto the deck. "I have coffee all set up outside. Trying to enjoy the last few warm days before the cold settles in." Her southern drawl crept into her speech. "Carla, I'm glad you came."

Carla gave a slight nod as she followed them outside. *So, she's nervous, too. She always talks in that damn accent when she's nervous or trying to impress someone – or both.* Her mom's deck overlooked the harbor, with Eastern Point Lighthouse across the water on the other side. Pockets of autumn color caught the sunlight as defiant leaves clung to trees not yet barren. Envy bubbled up inside as she took in the view. "Must be nice to be able to afford a place like this."

Betty Sue handed her a steaming mug of coffee, turning to appreciate the colors. "I've been comfortable here. I looked at a bigger townhouse over on Eastern Point, but liked this view better."

"Of *course,* you looked at a bigger spot." Words tumbled out of Carla's mouth before she could stop them. "Maybe you liked this one because it was farther away from Nonna and me."

Betty Sue opened her mouth to protest, but stopped herself. "If I'm being honest – and I'm trying to be – you're right. When I moved back, I didn't want to give up my independence, and—"

Carla resisted throwing her mug over the railing into the trees. "But you had no problem with me having *none*, did you? You'd pop in for your weekly visit and then tell all your friends how you moved back home to take care of your dear old mother!"

"Look, I don't want to rehash all my mistakes tonight, okay?"

"Yeah, well it's not that easy to forget from where I'm standing," Carla scoffed. "Did you ever *once* think about throwing a few dollars our way?" She tried to conceal the shaking in her voice. "Do you have *any* idea how much easier it might have been for Nonna and me with a little financial support?"

She waited for her mother to return the barb – as she always did – but instead found the silence almost maddening. "What? You've got nothing to say?"

Betty Sue stood quietly, meeting her gaze, but without the fire in her eyes. "I don't want to keep doing this. I've apologized over and over, and I'll continue. But I can't go back and change anything. Tell me what you want *now,* and I'll try to show you that I want things to be different between us."

Carla wanted to lash out, but recalled Jean's words. *The only way things are going to change is if you do something different than you've been doing all these years. Damn it! I don't know how to do that!*

Jean sensed Carla's apprehension and intervened. "Betty Sue, I told Carla about your work with the new foundation, so she's aware of your attempts to make amends. She actually has something she *does* need, and I think now's a perfect time for her to ask." She stared directly at Carla. "Don't *you?*"

Carla glared at her neighbor, trying to ignore the churning in her stomach.

"What is it?" Betty Sue asked. "Please," she pleaded. "Tell me."

Carla's words stumbled out of her mouth. "It's about the bar... there's renovations I want to do—"

"Of course!" Betty Sue interrupted. "I'll get my checkbook and give you whatever you want!"

"No!" Carla's reply stopped her mother after one step. "I don't want you to write me a check!"

"But you just said—"

"I didn't say I wanted your money. I don't *ever* want to owe you anything, got it?"

"It would be a *gift*," Betty Sue's voice was cold. "So, what then? What did you come to ask me?"

Carla's confidence wavered, and her voice was almost a whisper. "I...want you to cosign a loan for me. I can guarantee you'll never have to pay a penny, but I couldn't get it on my own."

"Well, I could call Dennis at the bank, and I'm sure they'd—"

"I don't want you to *call* anyone, okay? I don't want you to try and control how this plays out. If you don't wanna sign, that's fine. I have someone else who will."

Betty Sue saw the glance toward Jean. "So...you're gonna be the fairy godmother? It'll always be you, won't it? She's always going to think of you as her mom, no matter what I do to try and change."

"That's because she's always *been* my mom!" Carla spewed. "For God's sake, can't you just be grateful I had someone to turn to?"

"I will always be here for *both* of you, damn it!" Jean tried to diffuse the tension. "Yes, I'm glad I could give Carla the love and support she needed over the years – but there's nothing I'd love more than to see the two of you build some kind of relationship. So please...can you help her with what she's asked you for, and nothing more right now?"

All three stood listening to the surf, as mother and daughter grappled with taking that leap of faith, knowing it would change their relationship going forward.

In the end, it was Betty Sue who found Carla's gaze. "I would be happy...to cosign your loan." Her voice faltered, waiting for a response.

Carla fought the apprehension and willed herself to speak, even though her tongue was like sandpaper in her mouth. "I've asked for fifty thousand, and I'll call the bank tomorrow and find out how to proceed."

"I'm sure they simply need my signature. And I'm hoping there's nothing wrong with Joey—"

"He's fine," Carla replied. "He's actually leaving the bar to me in his will, but he wants me to start running it now, so he can train me in the stuff I don't know yet."

Betty Sue's eyes were misty. "I can't think of anyone better qualified to take over the Keel. You'll do an awesome job. I almost wish I wasn't working with the foundation now – you'd be a real contender for one of their grants if we weren't related."

"About that," Carla said. "Why, all of a sudden, are you giving your money away to women you've never met – when you never gave me or Nonna a penny?"

Betty Sue teared up as she looked out on the harbor. "Maybe to try and wash away some of the guilt? I've spent a lot of time feeling guilty for abandoning you, and hope I can keep other women from thinking the only way to get ahead is to leave this town. I've read their applications, and can relate to how they feel trapped."

"What the hell does that mean?" Carla scoffed.

Betty Sue leaned against the railing and inhaled the salt air to quiet her racing heart. "When I was young...I hated the fish factory, but didn't see a future anywhere else back then."

"Yeah, right, Mom. Did you forget how Nonna worked her butt off so you could go to secretarial school instead? Little did she know you'd run off with your boss and leave us."

"Sometimes..." Betty Sue's voice broke. "I almost wish she hadn't. I might have been happier."

"Oh, please, spare me the drama!" Carla found the old patterns of communication so much easier.

"I couldn't wait to get out of this town, and now...now I wish I'd never left."

"But you *did*," Carla spit out. "And you had no trouble trading in your seven year old daughter for all that money."

"That's true...and yet you're far better off than I'll ever be."

"Excuse me?" Carla stood up, ready to storm out again. "You dare to say that, with all your millions in the bank?!"

"Look where it's gotten me!" Betty Sue said. "I look at you – with Paul and Joey, and Jean and the neighbors who grew up with me in the Fort. They still have their kids living right here, and they'll have their grandkids here, too, because they know family and community are more valuable than all the money in the world." She met Carla's gaze with tears in her eyes. "I think you've learned that now, too."

Carla opened her mouth to respond, but the barb remained unspoken as her mother's words settled. She glanced over at Jean, then rose and walked out on to the deck, breathing in the salt air and fighting back tears. *Who does she think she is, preaching about family and community? She doesn't know anything!* Thoughts of Nonna, Jean, and Joey over the years flooded her mind, revealing the truth her mother spoke. Images of Paul and Brad joined the others, filling her heart with another layer of love. *I hate that she's right. I can't imagine what life would be without any of them – my chosen family, who make this place feel like home now.*

Jean had slipped out to stand beside her, wrapping an arm around her shoulder. "You okay?"

"Not sure," she choked out.

"Somehow," Jean whispered, "I think Nonna really wanted you to just be here tonight with an open mind."

Carla glanced inside at an empty couch. "Where did she go?"

"She said she'd be in her room. Thought you needed your *other* mom more right now."

With Jean's arms enfolding her, Carla let the tears flow. "I...just don't...I'm scared to make room for her...it still hurts so much..."

Jean gently lifted Carla's chin to meet her gaze. "Honey, that hurt's never gonna heal if you don't face it and deal with it. The only way to do that is to meet her half way – even if it's baby steps."

"But how can I trust her after all this time?"

"You can't. It takes time to build that bridge."

Carla's stomach churned. "What if you're wrong? What if it doesn't work?"

"Then you'll find peace in knowing you tried." Jean stepped back and met her gaze. "But what if I'm right?"

Carla leaned on the railing, looking up at the stars. *Oh, Nonna, what the hell do I do? I wouldn't even know where to start.*

Jean surmised her thoughts, and offered help. "You and Paul are coming over to eat next week. I could easily add a plate." She kissed Carla's forehead and went back inside, knowing Carla needed time to think.

A few minutes passed before Carla followed, and she walked past Betty Sue's bedroom on the way to the door. Her hand reached for the knob, but she swallowed hard and turned around to find her mom coming out of her room.

Their eyes met, and time stretched out in the silence between them before Carla found words. "Paul and I are having Thanksgiving dinner at Jean's." Her eyes dropped, not having the strength to maintain eye contact. Her voice was almost a whisper. "You can join us if you want."

Betty Sue replied, her own voice also shaky. "I'd like that very much."

Carla gave a slight nod, then walked out the door, eager to find security in her car. *One baby step, Nonna. It's all I can take right now – but I did it. Please don't let me fall, okay?* She drove in silence along the harbor, past the beach she'd grown up on, and back into her neighborhood. She knew every house, and every person behind each door. The closer she got to home, the louder her mom's words echoed in her head. *Family and community. Even without my mom or dad, I had both of those things here in the Fort. Now I have to find out if I can add the parents I never had back into my life – into my family. God, Nonna – help me.*

# CHAPTER TWENTY-SEVEN

Carla crossed the street early on Thanksgiving morning to help in the kitchen. She greeted Hannah and Kim who were peeling potatoes and squash, and Jean at the counter draping some foil over a small turkey. "Morning, sunshine...wanna open the oven door for me? This guy is ready to go."

"Happy to oblige...and hungry already." She held the door open as Jean slid the roasting pan into the oven, and then closed it for her. "So put me to work. What do you need?"

"Why don't I help Kim finish up the veggies, and you and Hannah can go in and set the dining room table up?"

"Works for me."

Hannah left her knife on the cutting board and held up orange fingers. "Let me wash my hands first; it's the one thing I hate about cutting squash."

Carla spotted the dish of cut celery. "Mind if I steal one?"

"You can have two if you guarantee a pan of lasagna is coming back here later on," Kim replied with a grin.

"All set and ready to go," Carla assured before crunching on the celery. "I'll heat it up over there and Paul can carry it."

"So, is he nervous about your mom being here?"

"Not as nervous as I am. I'm so afraid I'll slip up and mention my dad during dinner. I'm definitely not ready for *that* confrontation."

"Everyone knows the ground rules," Jean said. "No one brings up his name today."

Hannah finished drying her hands and also grabbed a piece of celery. "But right now, you can tell us if you talked to him this week."

Carla smiled. "He called Wednesday night and we talked a bit. I'm gonna call him later on this morning."

"Does he even celebrate the holiday today?" Kim asked, finishing up the last potato.

"No, Canada celebrates Thanksgiving in October. He's working today, trying to finish up his current job so he can head back for another visit."

"I can't imagine there's much work in Peggy's Cove in the middle of winter."

Carla chuckled. "There's not much of *anything* in Peggy's Cove in winter – except cold."

Hannah tugged on Carla's shirt. "Come on, you – let's get the table done."

"Yeah, you can talk about your *boyfriends,*" Kim teased.

"Sounds good to me," Carla replied. She followed Hannah into the dining room. "Is JJ gonna make it today, or is the warden keeping him home?"

Hannah laughed at the nickname JJ had given his father. "They're having dinner at one, so he should arrive by dessert. He wants to be there for his mom one last time."

"Has he told them he's moving to Peg's yet?"

Hannah shook her head as they cleared items off the table. "Not until next week, after his court hearing. Once he's officially cleared from community service and the case is closed, he'll pack up pretty quickly, I think."

"And what about *you?* Getting excited about him not having any more curfews?"

Hannah blushed. "It's all I think about lately. I can't wait to rip his clothes off for the first time."

"Look at us," Carla said. "Almost thirty years old, and we're gushing like teenagers."

"No one I'd rather share all this with."

"Me, neither. You're like a sister and a bestie all rolled up in one."

"Ditto. Now grab that tablecloth on the hutch," Hannah said. "Mom has all the dishes stacked up and ready."

They chatted as they worked, sharing a task they'd done almost every year. When they finished, Hannah added a simple autumn centerpiece with candles and silk flowers.

As Carla watched, her eyes grew misty. "Thanks for that. I remember Nonna picking that out a few years ago at the fall craft fair to bring along. That was her last healthy year."

"She's still here, Bestie. And she'll help you through today; I know she wants nothing more than to have you start over with your mom."

Carla sighed. "Well, I'll need all the help I can get." She gazed around the table. "So where exactly is she gonna sit? And how far away from me can it be?"

Hannah grinned, reaching for a small stack of seating cards behind her. "I've got you covered. She's sitting next to my mom at one end, and I have Kim to her left. Paul will sit on my mom's right, and you'll be next to him, with me at the other end."

Carla watched her as placed a card at each setting. "Opposite ends, with you and Paul on either side of me...yeah, I think that's about as safe as I can be. So, who is the extra seat for?"

"Vinny's coming; Kim invited him, and I thought he and JJ would enjoy getting to know each other since they'll be living across the hall from each other before long."

"I thought maybe she might have invited Bill."

"Yeah, right...believe me, if that day comes, I'll shout it from the rooftops. I'm just glad it's not the dorky organist that's been asking her out. He's such a snob."

"Who's a snob?" Kim asked, carrying some trivets in from the kitchen.

"Edwaaard Pennington," Hannah said, standing tall with her nose in the air.

Kim scoffed. "Now I'm glad I didn't ask him to come today."

"Like he'd want to come and eat with the common people," Hannah retorted.

Carla joined in the fun. "Yeah, especially with a gay man and another with a criminal record. So why *didn't* you have the fancy professor join us?"

"I thought about inviting him – but he told me he'd be heading down to have dinner with his parents on Beacon Hill, so I didn't bother."

"Beacon Hill. I rest my case," Hannah said.

Kim placed the last trivet on the table. "Yeah, well, you might have to get used to him. I'm ready to start dating again, and there's not a whole lot of other options out there right now."

"Oh, I beg to differ," Carla replied. "I think it's a bummer that you're so against hanging out with Bill. He and Paul have gotten to be good friends, and we could have had quite the party today."

Kim met her gaze, and her voice softened. "I didn't know that. I'm glad he's found another friend. I know he misses Anthony, too."

"Rumor has it," Carla continued, "that he might not be a fisherman too much longer—"

"What do you mean? Is Nate okay?"

"He's slowing down; Bill doesn't think he's gonna be able to manage the boat much longer."

"I know Terri's shared her concerns with Hannah; I can't imagine either of them doing anything else after all these years."

Carla's eyes twinkled. "Well, Bill and Paul have some ideas for the not so distant future – and none of them include fishing – just in case that makes any kind of difference."

"How about we concentrate on today," Kim said, "and how you're gonna manage dinner with your mother."

"The lady knows how to change the subject," Hannah replied. "Besides, I have *you* sitting next to Betty Sue, so be ready to talk her ear off if things start to heat up. And remember – *no* mention of Brad."

"Fine. I'll keep quiet about Brad if you guys lay off about Bill – how's that?"

"Fair trade," Carla said with a slight nod. She glanced at the clock. "And I better get my butt back across the street before Paul shows up. I have a lasagna to put together. See you both later on...we'll be back before dinner."

Hannah gave her friend a hug. "Have a nice chat with your dad, and don't let Paul distract you so much that you forget about the lasagna."

Carla laughed. "You kidding? I wouldn't have a chance today; he's been talking about that lasagna all week." She scooted out the door after yelling a quick good bye to Jean in the kitchen, and looked forward to talking to one parent, while trying to calm her nerves about facing the other.

Less than an hour later, her phone signaled that her dad had beat her to the call.

"I figured you'd be up by now if there's a turkey involved; I hope I'm not interrupting meal prep, but wanted to say hello."

"Morning, Dad." Carla couldn't help but smile as she got used to using the word "dad" in her vocabulary. "I was across the street earlier and can verify that the bird's in the oven, and the lasagna is all ready to pop in here when the time is right."

"I thought you might be a little stressed with dinner only a few hours away."

"My stomach's been in knots since I woke up. I don't how to be around her without fighting; it's all we've ever done since she moved back here."

"Hey, you've already taken the hardest step – the invitation alone was the step you needed to take. Now it's just baby steps."

"To where, though?" Carla had curled up on the couch, thinking of how Rufus would climb up for a head scratch during Brad's visit. "I can't imagine we'll ever have a normal mother-daughter relationship."

"What's normal?" her dad asked. "Besides, you can make the relationship anything you need it to be. Even if it's only cordial civility."

Carla laughed. "I like that term – although I suspect the civil will come easier than the cordial."

"When do you go to the bank to finalize the loan?"

"Monday morning. And then I head to work and convince Joey to actually close down for a month to get the bulk of the work done."

"You've already discussed all that – and I know he's ready to let you take the reins."

"Well, it's one thing to be ready and another to actually do it. The Keel has been his baby since the beginning, and I wonder what he'll do when we start taking ripping his floor up."

"So, I wanted to talk to you about that; have you chosen a contractor yet?"

"I talked to a few, but no decision yet. I wanted the money in the bank before I made any definite decisions."

"How would you feel about some free labor?"

Carla's heart quickened. "What do you mean?"

"I didn't want to say anything until I knew I could pull it off, but if you'll have me, I can do the work for nothing – except for maybe room and board for a bit."

"Are you kidding? You'd come down to do the job?"

"While I was up finishing this one job, I was also passing off a few other smaller jobs to friends. I can be there sometime next week and be ready to start if supplies are easy to find."

"Oh my God," Carla exclaimed. "Yes! I can't imagine anyone else I'd rather have do the work!"

"Are you sure you're okay with me staying at the house, though? I don't want to get in the way of what you're building with Paul."

"Paul knows how important you are; I think he'd be fine. I'll talk to him when he gets here. But are you sure? Like, I'm not taking you away from jobs you need for bills or anything?"

Brad laughed. "You really have no idea how dead it is here in winter; it's actually easier to close the house down for a month than keep it heated on the money I bring in."

"Will you be able to get everything done here in a month? And will you need some help?"

"That's something I was gonna ask you. I might be able to use a little help if you want the place open for January. Do you think any of the local contractors might be interested in some small jobs?"

"Oh, my God – I know the perfect person to help you!" Carla shared JJ's situation with Brad, and was thrilled by his enthusiastic reply.

"I'll ask him today at dinner," Carla began. "Oh, crap! I can't do that – not with my mother sitting at the other end of the table." Brad didn't answer for a second. "You still there?"

"Yeah, I was mulling that over...and maybe it's the perfect time."

"Are you kidding? You want me to let it out that you've not only been down here, but that you're coming back? For a month? Are you crazy?"

"I'm sure there are plenty of Thanksgiving celebrations that have far more drama than that." Brad's voice didn't slow down Carla's racing heart. "Sometimes it's best to simply rip the band-aid off. It's not like she's not going to find out at *some* point."

"Why should she? Just because she's cosigning the loan, it doesn't give her any right to know anything about what I do with the money – or who I hire."

"That's not what I'm trying—"

"It's none of her business! I don't want her to know anything about you being around!"

Once again, a long pause preceded Brad's reply. "What exactly are you afraid of right now? I can hear it in your voice."

*She doesn't deserve to know! She'll just try to steal you away from me and then I'll be alone again.*

"Carla? Come on, talk to me."

"Why would you even want her to know you're back?" she blurted out. "After all she put you through, and all the alcohol...why even bother?"

"Is that what you're afraid of? That I might start drinking again? I can promise you, that's not—"

"How do you know? I know what she's like, Dad. Her last boyfriend ended up in jail, and she'd probably jump at the chance to try and get her hooks into you again. And...I don't wanna share, okay?"

"So *that's* it...sounds like you're more worried I might dive into a relationship than you are about me picking up the bottle again."

Carla wiped the tears forming. "Why would you even want to be around the woman who caused you so much pain?"

"Maybe for the same reason you are." Brad's voice was quiet. "You're not the only one who has skeletons to let go of, kiddo."

"But...what if you can't?"

"Look, I know I have a bunch of unresolved issues with your mother. And some of them scare the hell outta me – but I'd rather face them head on instead of trying to hide and pretend they don't exist. It's only a matter of time before we run into each other, and I'd rather be in control of that situation."

"I'm...just afraid, I guess. I've never been able to trust her, and I don't know how I'm gonna build it if I see her using her Southern Belle charm on you."

"Sounds like maybe you're just afraid I'd choose her over you."

A tear escaped down Carla's cheek. "I don't wanna lose you again."

"I can promise you that's never gonna happen," Brad replied. "I mean that. Nothing's gonna come between me and my daughter ever again. Nothing. Or no one."

"It's just...I know how much you loved her. And how easy it might be for her to—"

"Don't you think I've thought about all that? How much I'd have to lose? Trust me, kiddo, when the time comes, I'll be clutching that sobriety coin in my pocket when I finally meet up with her. Hell, I might even take it out and flash it in her face--like garlic and Dracula."

Carla laughed. "Sounds pretty accurate to me."

"Besides, I have a far more potent weapon than garlic to keep me sober."

"What's that?"

"You, silly. So, make my day. March over there later on and announce my impending arrival. Shock the hell out of her. Then you can tell me about all the drama later on. How does that sound?"

"Sounds like I'll shock the hell out of more than just her – I've spent a week making sure everyone promised to keep your name quiet."

"Even better. You'll have total control of how she finds out, and I suspect you'll enjoy having the upper hand. Just don't forget to ask JJ about the job, okay?"

Carla heard Paul's truck pulling in to the driveway. "I won't – and I'll fill you in later. Paul's just pulling in, so I'll say goodbye for now. Happy Thanksgiving, Dad."

"Best one ever with you back in my life. Now go and make it memorable for everyone."

Carla filled Paul in her conversation with Brad as the lasagna heated up, and he gave his approval of her dinner plan.

"I think waiting until dessert is a great idea," he said. "That way, if things get too crazy, I can drag you outta there if I have to without disrupting too much of dinner."

"Not sure how much I'll eat...my stomach will be churning through the whole meal."

Paul laughed. "I've watched you eat through all kinds of stress. I don't think your stomach is any match for turkey and lasagna. But I think your dad is right about taking control of the situation. And I for one can't *wait* to see her face when you drop the bomb."

"Oh my, God – what if she decides not to cosign the loan? Maybe I should wait—"

"Why would she?" Paul replied. "If anything, she might be more willing to do so, if only to find out more about the one she sent away."

"I hadn't thought of it that way. God, she might start grilling me to find out everything I know about him."

Paul pulled her in for a hug. "And you don't owe her anything in that department. In fact, I would encourage you to stay *out* of whatever interactions they encounter; what happens between them is out of your control – or should be, at least.”

“Might be easier said than done.”

“Well,” Paul whispered, running his fingers down her spine until she shivered. “I know another relationship you could concentrate on instead.” He kissed her deeply, and she eagerly responded. “So how much time do we have before the lasagna’s done?”

She began unbuckling his belt with a grin. “Enough.”

———

Dinner proved to be less awkward than Carla thought it might be. Betty Sue conversed more with Jean and Kim at the other end of the table, although responded warmly when Paul shared anecdotes of growing up in Maine and how much he enjoyed being in Gloucester.

“It sounds like you’re thinking about staying in Gloucester long term,” Betty Sue said.

“You couldn’t drag me away at this point,” Paul replied, reaching under the table to squeeze Carla’s thigh. “Everything I want in life is right here.”

Carla’s heart swelled, remembering their earlier love making. *How did I get so damn lucky? You could have walked into any bar for a drink that night, and you chose the Keel.*

Carla met her mother’s gaze, and actually smiled. Paul had brought so much love and confidence into her life, and she could feel the animosity toward her mother slowly melting away. *Maybe there’s hope for us yet. As long as you stay away from my dad.*

The doorbell interrupted her thoughts, and Hannah’s eyes lit up as she almost bolted for the door. Carla watched their embrace before Hannah led him into the dining room, and she briefly remembered how she’d been so hung up on JJ in the past, even trying to keep Hannah from dating him because of her own jealousy. *And look how perfect they are for each other. And how happy I am for both of them now that Paul’s taught me what real love is.*

She let JJ and Vinny talk awhile about his upcoming move to Peg’s, feeling her stomach starting to churn a bit as the big reveal approached. Paul must have sensed her nervousness, as he leaned back in his seat and placed his hand gently on her back.

"You've got this," he whispered in her ear, gently running his fingers down her spine like he had earlier in the day.

Carla took a sip of wine, glancing down at her mom talking to Jean before addressing JJ.

"So, I heard you telling Vinny you're looking for a job at this point. Find anything yet?"

JJ finished his bite of pumpkin pie before responding. "I had a second interview over at the Spinnaker shop. It's not exactly what I wanna do, but right now I'll take whatever I can to cover my bills over at Peg's."

"Well, if they should offer you the job, I'd like to talk to you first about another possibility."

By now, most conversation had stopped, and Carla knew it was time. "How would you feel about spending a month working on the renovations at the Keel? I can't give you benefits or anything, but you'd have a salary at least."

"Seriously? I mean, I'd love that – but I'm not sure I could take on a job that big without—"

"You wouldn't be alone. I actually have a contractor all lined up, but he said he'd really like some help."

"Wouldn't he have someone already?"

Carla took a deep breath as she noticed nervous eyes around the table. *They have no idea. And I might be crazy, but here goes nothing.* "He actually needs someone local to work with him, as he's traveling a distance to help me out." She kept her mother's face in her peripheral vision as she continued. "He's coming down from Canada for a while. It's my dad – Brad Douglas."

The effect was as she expected it to be, with Betty Sue's reaction magnified by the surprise of everyone who had worked so hard to avoid the topic of Brad throughout the meal.

*"Brad?"* Betty Sue blurted out. "Coming here? How in the world did that—"

"I tracked him down on social media – well, Hannah did – and he responded right away when I reached out."

"But to ask him to come and do your renovations? After years of not seeing each other? I mean, you were a toddler when he left here—"

"He's already been down to visit, Mother. Just a couple of weeks ago."

"He was...*here?* In Gloucester?"

Carla nodded. "He stayed for a couple of weeks. We spent lots of time together, getting to know each other...and he's a carpenter, and wants to come back down to do the job for me."

Complete silence hung in the air, with everyone waiting for Betty Sue's reaction.

Her mom stared down at her plate for a few moments before looking up at Carla. Her voice cracked as she spoke. "I suspect... Nonna's letter had something to do with all this?"

Carla nodded, without speaking. Part of her wanted to lash out and let her mother have it again about sending her father away, but she leaned on the other part. The one that was slowly learning to open up and take risks. The one Paul had helped to find.

Betty Sue's lip quivered, her voice almost a whisper. "I'm...I imagine that was quite the reunion. I'm happy for you, Carla. You deserve a chance to know him."

Carla hadn't any idea on what to expect from her mom, but it surely wasn't this. A quiet, almost genuine, affirmation. *What the hell? I was expecting an explosion – and instead, you're sitting there all demure. What the hell are you thinking? Or planning inside?*

She spoke tentatively, trying out new words she'd never used with her mother. Honest words. Maybe even vulnerable words.

"It was a great visit. And I'm looking forward to having him back, to pick up where we left off." Still nothing. She sensed, for the first time, that Betty Sue was genuinely trying to meet her half way. *If she has other motives, at least for now, she's hiding them well.* And for now, that was enough.

# CHAPTER TWENTY-NINE

Carla waited for Betty Sue outside the bank Monday morning to sign the final papers for the loan. She'd have the money in her account by the end of the week, and renovations could start as soon as Brad came back down. *Will she bring him up today? Maybe she wanted me alone to drill me for information. Or maybe, just maybe, she really IS trying to change.*

"Good morning! It sure is a chilly one!" Betty Sue approached, wrapping her winter coat a little tighter around her body. She had a matching scarf and beret hat, and wore light gloves. Carla, who had grabbed a simple sweatshirt when she left the house, laughed.

"That's what you get for living in Tennessee all those years. This is nothing for us locals."

"What can I say? I got used to the sunshine and warmer weather. Maybe I should have moved to Florida instead of coming back here."

"You still could – nothing's stopping you."

Betty Sue opened her mouth to reply, but paused before speaking. "I'm not sure how to take that comment. Usually, it's an opener to bite my head off after I reply."

"Relax. I'm making an observation, nothing more. And for the record, it's just as awkward for me knowing what to say after years of doing nothing but arguing."

Betty Sue smiled. "Awkward as it is, I must admit I kind of like this new attempt at being civil." She opened the door. "Shall we?"

A teller escorted them into Taylor Grayson's office. The woman stood to greet them, this time with a warm and welcoming demeanor. "Betty Sue, how nice to see you again. Dennis would have been here to say hello, but had a meeting over in Essex. He sends his best. Please – both of you – have a seat."

*So, this is how the rich are treated – all gushy and superficial, while I got stern looks over the top of her reading glasses.*

"Ms. Douglas, we have the paperwork all drawn up for your loan. We'll just need a couple of signatures to make it official." She turned to Betty Sue. "Are you sure about being a cosigner?"

*Really? You're gonna look down on me again? And make it easy for my mother to hold this over me? Maybe I should have insisted on Jean being the—*

"Quite honestly, Taylor, I'm a little disappointed that I need to be here at all."

Carla heard her mother's reply, and was immediately ready to fight again. However, before she could open her mouth to speak her mind, her mother continued, and for once, she was grateful she had held her tongue.

"Why you didn't think that Carla could handle this loan on her own is a mystery to me. I have never known anyone who has worked harder for every penny she's earned. Over the years, she has held down one – sometimes two – jobs, to make sure her grandmother was taken care of. She singlehandedly paid the bills, helped to run a local business, and was the sole caregiver for a grandmother with dementia. Even when I returned back home, she never asked for a dime. And I have to ask, in all that time, did a single check of hers ever come back with insufficient funds? Ever?"

Carla had to bite the inside of her cheek to keep from tearing up. Hearing her mother stand up for her – even berate the bank for how they treated her – was a whole new experience. She sat dumbfounded, not knowing whether to laugh or cry. *It's like I don't even know who you are anymore. But I think I like this version.*

Taylor Grayson looked down at the desk and shuffled the loan papers around, her cheeks flushed with embarrassment. "I was only following bank policy, Ms. Marino. So, I assume that's a yes in terms of being a willing cosigner."

"Well, I wouldn't *be* here if I wasn't absolutely willing." She grabbed a pen and signed her name with flourish before handing the pen back across the desk. "But I can guarantee my signature was not necessary. I'm confident Carla will bring the Even Keel back to the popularity it had when I was growing up, and pay that loan off early – all without ever needing a penny from me." She met Carla's gaze and her voice softened. "I mean every word of that."

Carla accepted the pen being held out toward her, and had to blink back tears to see the line where her signature was required. She placed the pen quietly on the desk, and sat back in disbelief.

"Well," Taylor said, flipping the loan back to the front page. "That takes care of everything at this end. You should see the money in your new account within three to five business days. Is there anything else we can help you with this morning?"

Carla fought the urge to speak her mind, and instead reached out to shake the banker's hand. "No, I think everything's been said that needed to be. Thank you for your time, but I need to get to work at this point."

"I'll walk out with you," Betty Sue said, gathering her coat and gloves. "Taylor, thank you for your assistance, and please give my best to Dennis in return." Turning to Carla, she continued. "Shall we?"

Once outside, she took her time to find the right words. "I, um… thank you – for what you said in there. You didn't have to, but it was appreciated."

Betty Sue's voice wasn't nearly as confident as it had been inside. "I know you have every reason to doubt me right now, but I really am trying. Working with the women I'm meeting through the foundation makes me so much more aware of how badly I failed you for so long – and I only hope that you'll keep giving me the chance to make amends."

"It's still…kind of weird, that's all. It's gonna take some time."

"I'll take whatever time you give me, but will never try to push. That I can promise."

"No offense, Mom, but I don't think we're at the 'making promises' stage yet."

"Noted."

"I'm heading back over to the bar to celebrate with Joey...you can come along – if you'd like."

Betty Sue reached out to touch her daughter's arm. "This is your baby – and I meant what I said about not intruding. I'm only the silent cosigner. You go on...celebrate with Joey and start telling him how you're gonna run the place."

Carla chuckled. "Thank you again for this."

Betty Sue turned to leave, but stopped. "One more thing. I can assure you that I won't make excuses to stop in during renovations. And I won't try to reach out to Brad, even though I'd love to know how he's doing and apologize to him as well."

"Now *that* statement has me ready to lash out with our typical banter."

"I mean it, Carla. It was because of me that you were robbed of all those years with your father. I have no place – and no right – to take any of that time away. Give Joey my love."

With that, she turned and headed back down the street. Carla watched her go, wondering how long she'd question every statement her mother made. *Please, Nonna, I want to believe her. I want to see the changes she's making and know they're genuine. I don't know if we'll ever have a real mother-daughter bond, but for once I'm starting to think we might be able to have some kind of relationship. And I know that's just you watching over me – like you always will.*

With a light heart, she drove the short distance over to the bar, noting the faded sign out front. *The Even Keel. This place sure has been my even keel, giving me the balance and stability I needed to grow up – along with my chosen family.* She looked up at the sign and smiled as she got out of her car. "I promise you a new paint job and new lights in the next month or so."

Heading inside, she stopped short to find not just Joey, but Jean,

Hannah, JJ, Paul, and Bill at the counter with balloons and a cake box. Even Rod and Bernie joined in the festivities from their stools at the end, toasting her with held up beer mugs.

"What the hell?" She looked at Joey with tears in her eyes. "Did you set this up?"

The old man held open his arms and gave her a big hug. "Guess I gotta start calling *you* Boss now, huh? And for the record, it wasn't me."

Carla turned to Hannah, and then Paul who both shook their heads.

"Then who?"

From the kitchen, a familiar voice spoke. "It was me." Brad stepped out and smiled. "Had to be here for your big day." Carla welcomed his embrace as everyone cheered. She didn't even try to hide her tears until she stepped back.

"Wait? How did you get back down here so fast? I talked to you Saturday!"

Brad grinned. "I was already on the ferry when you called. Stayed over at Long Beach last night."

"I don't know what to say – except you guys are all the best."

"Hey, Squirt, he brought you something – I asked him to do a custom job for the occasion." Joey reached down below the bar and slowly lifted up a hand carved sign that said "Carla's Place" on it. "What do you say? I think it's time to replace the old sign outside, don't you?"

"I don't know Joey... this will always be the Even Keel to me."

"Tell ya what...we'll take that one down and hang it in the back room as a reminder of where you've come from. But from here on in, I want this community to know it's Carla's Place now, and see where you take it into the future. Deal?"

Carla ran her fingers over the beautiful letters that her dad had created. "Deal. And thank you. Both of you."

Hannah handed her a knife. "Now cut this damn cake and let's get this party started, shall we? JJ and your dad can schedule their first official meeting on the renovations, and you and Joey can fight over how long the place will be closed – but right now, let's just celebrate!"

Paul snuck up behind her as she reached out to open the cake box and wrapped his arms around her.

"Just so you know, I ordered the cake. Picked out the perfect message, if I do say so myself."

Carla opened the box, and put the knife down to give him a big kiss. Jean picked up the knife to take over. "Yup – that's perfect it is. Nice job, Paul."

Everyone craned their necks to read the words, and a collective "aww" was all the confirmation Carla needed. In blue icing, with waves and seagull decorations, the message stated what Carla had come to believe completely: HOME IS WHERE THE HEART IS.

There are several more stories to be told from Harbor Cove, but each one will focus on just one or two storylines. Next up?

Kelly and Travis will finally have a chance to reconnect. Will their marriage survive, or will other forces work against their efforts? Along the way, she'll have plenty of support from the brunch club as they all tackle their own issues.

As for a tentative date, I can't make any promises. With caregiving responsibilities increasing at home, my writing often has to be put aside. Know that I'll keep plodding along and will keep you informed through my mailing list. As for the second storyline, I'll let my readers decide! Keep an eye out for polls where YOU can choose who comes next!

Finally, if you enjoy this story, please consider leaving a quick review online. Thanks so much

# ACKNOWLEDGMENTS

To Noel Sellon, cover designer, who takes my jumbled ideas and images and creates magic every time!

To my sister, Cheryl, who has listened to my rants and frustrations throughout the process. Thanks for always being there and sharing the challenges of aging!

To my wonderful critique partners – Michele, Jo, and Janice. Thanks for your continued support and wise insights along the entire pathway to publication.

To my fellow writers, who encourage me, understand me, and remind me to never stop believing in my dreams.

To my own brunch club friends—I honestly couldn't get through life without you. A few of you might recognize yourselves in special "cameo characters" who portray your wonderful characteristics!

To my students — for allowing me to share a piece of myself as I used this current work to illustrate many of the steps taken as an indie author. I can't wait to someday read some of your published works!

To my readers – thank you for your patience on this one. It took a long time, but I trust that you'll enjoy your return to Gloucester!

Finally, to Bob, Beth, and Rebecca – as always, you are my heart and my home.

# ABOUT THE AUTHOR

Laurel Wenson's love of small-town life serves as inspiration for her stories about love and friendship that span generations – and always promise a happy ending. *Home is Where the Heart Is* follows *The Harbor Cover Brunch Club*, set in the fishing town of Gloucester, MA, where six middle-aged women and their families rely on each other throughout life's challenges.

The author has also written the Caldwell series for young adults (which older women love as well): *A Promise to Keep, A Heart to Heal, A Family to Cherish, & A Place to Belong.*

Her first book, *Sets on a Shoestring*, is a non-fiction guidebook for children's theater production.

Laurel lives in Bethlehem, PA, with her husband, two daughters, and a frisky feline. She is a member of the Greater Lehigh Valley Writers Group and an avid participant in National Novel Writing Month. She self-published her first book at age 60, proving it's never too late to pursue a dream!

Follow her on social media or visit her website at: laurelwenson.com

Paperbacks can be found at Barnes & Noble or Amazon; e-books exclusively on Amazon.

Contact the author for a signed copy: laurelwenson@gmail.com

www.ingramcontent.com/pod-product-compliance
Lightning Source LLC
Chambersburg PA
CBHW070354200726
48294CB00003B/904